The Duck Pond Incident

Charlie Humphries

ISBN 978-1-912700-94-3

Book designed and edited by: Ian Sharman

www.markosia.com

First Edition

CONTENTS

We Should All Learn Sign Language

Morgan was sure that if daisies weren't so beautiful or charming they would have been classed as a weed because of their new-found refusal to just die. No, instead, half of Morgan's working day in the cemetery was spent cutting them back. They were pretty, sure. Somebody was coming in and planting more of them after curfew. However, between lying awake in the complete dark, punctuated by the occasional dying satellite, and worrying over every tiny noise outside, Morgan was thankful for this one mercy. At least daisies were gentle on the eyes after the short walk between their home and work, through what had been.

Today would have been July 15th 2313, if people still kept precise dates: the only thing people counted and observed were the sunrises until the water rations were due or until the slow creep of winter would kill off their carefully tended vegetable plots. Morgan peeped through the gap in the curtain and breathed deep against the glass. In the surface fog they traced two words that had gained more meaning in the years since the government had taken the necessary steps to ensure the people were kept safe: Happy Birthday. Morgan allowed a small smile to prick the corners of their mouth before getting ready for work. They had ironed their blue work polo shirt specially for today, using up what little energy was left in the house-battery. They settled their baseball cap just so over their cropped dark hair - in need of a wash, truth be told - and allowed a small wink in the mirror before leaving the house. There was no point in locking the door: if people were desperate enough, they would smash a window. And Morgan couldn't afford to replace another broken window.

"Good morning, crew! How are we all?" Natasha grinned round at their tiny team, rocking back and forth on the balls of her feet. Her tightly braided blonde hair was pinned up under her work cap, her work shirt a little grubby from dirt and grass stains.

"Can't complain," George said with a smile. He saluted the group with his chipped mug of tea, and there were a few nods.

"Good, good, good! Now, before we move onto today's schedule, we have a very important thing to celebrate. Today is Morgan's birthday!" Natasha took her hands from behind her back and offered Morgan a rectangular parcel wrapped in Christmas paper. Morgan's eyes felt like they were going to pop out of their head. They placed a hand against their chest.

~For me?~ they mouthed.

"Yes! A little something from all of us. I'm sorry it's in Christmas paper. It's all I had left."

Morgan took the parcel between all eight fingers and two thumbs, unable to contain the grin that was spreading across their face. Pinching the corner of a strip of tape between thumb and forefinger, Morgan drew it away a millimeter at a time. Natasha, George and Carmen watched on, holding their breath.

Morgan closed their eyes and ripped the paper off in shreds.

"Hey, Nat, if this paper was the last of it, what'll you use at Christmas?" Carmen twirled a scrap of the shiny red and blue paper between her fingers. Natasha shrugged.

"I don't know. I'll think of something."

Morgan pulled the book out of its wrapping and gave it a grand sniff, hugged the book to their chest and looked around at their colleagues.

~Thank you.~

"You are most welcome, Morgan. Enjoy. And because it's your special day, I'm taking you off daisy duty. George has volunteered in your place. You'll be digging out a new vegetable plot down by the gate. As wide and long as you can manage. I wanted to attempt staples next year, onions and carrots."

Morgan placed their book on the trestle table with a gentle reverence and brushed an imaginary speck of lint from the cover before beginning to sign with their hands.

~We should attempt peppers and tomatoes too. Is the greenhouse still in one piece? We might have a better chance of germination in there.~

"You know, I've not checked." Natasha took her tiny notepad from her trouser pocket and the ever-present pencil from behind her ear and scribbled some notes.

"I'll go check it out while I'm hacking at the daisies," George said. He drained off his mug and rocked to his feet, his hip clicking. "I'm getting old," he laughed. Morgan wasn't sure how old George was exactly, but he was in his sixties at least. His hair was a mop of black and silver now that hair dye was no longer a vital commodity.

The team finished up in the chapel's small side room and went en masse to the tool shed tucked off to one side of the grounds in the shade of a hawthorn tree. Morgan skipped ahead, breathing in the sleepy buzz of the morning, the rising pollen and insects, the brash song of some hidden bird.

Only, something made Morgan stop mid-skip, flung their arms out to stop the others. Under the shadow of a hawthorn tree stood the small shed, squat and in need of a new coat of paint. The newest thing about it had been the padlock. Even the 'private' sign was rusting at the edges. But the padlock was on the ground, the shackle snapped clean in two.

"No, Morgan! Stay here! Morgan!"

They waved Natasha off, stepped towards the shiny lump of metal and crouched to pick it up. Morgan watched the shed, strained their ears for any sound out of place. And there, underneath the bird chorus, was a noise like whimpering. Morgan waved the others back and their shuffling and whispering was loud in the morning hush. Since everything had changed and rationing had become an ever-present pressure there had been stories of groups moving through towns and taking as they pleased. These stories were whispered during the witching hour but bloomed into a cautionary fairy tale when the sun burst over the horizon.

Morgan went to lick their lips, flinched at the thrashing stump in their parched mouth as they stepped closer. The book-joy had dissipated and was nothing more than a memory. Morgan took hold of the shed latch and wrenched the door open with a clatter. A cry from the gloom, heavy-weight shuffling as the body heaved itself backwards. A trail of blood.

"Rich?" came the whisper. Morgan's eyes adjusted to the gloom and took in the youth clutching their side, sprawled amongst tarps and wool skeins.

"Shit, shit, shit." The youth's breath came in sharp bursts. Morgan took a step into the shed, filling it, spilling over in anger. The tools were gone, the walls empty of their spades, hoes, rakes and secateurs. Morgan turned their gaze back on the intruder and bared their teeth.

"Morgan? We're coming in." George poked his head around the door and let out a sigh. "Oh, well now that's a shame." He shook his head and placed a hand where his spade used to hang.

"George! This woman needs looking at!"

Natasha hauled George out of the shed, shoved past Morgan and dropped to her knees beside the young woman.

"Maybe we should just call an ambulance." George looked wistfully around the door.

She had sustained a stab wound in the side, but Natasha couldn't see if the blade had been broken off or not. The young woman had already lost a lot of blood. Natasha frowned and had started to speak, but the youth cut her off.

"No hospitals, no police. My mates'll be back soon enough., They're just waiting for dark."

"What's your name, lass?"

"Don't you be lassing me mate."

George blushed deep.

~Her name is Susan.~ Morgan signed and looked straight at their guest, invader, thief.

"Shit, what's all that?"

~We should tip you on the compost heap and leave you to rot, like your friends have.~ Morgan's hands were nearly a blur, tears pricking their eyes and in the end they threw their hands up with a shout, burst out of the shed into the dappled sunlight, took deep gulping breaths with hands on knees. Breakfast was roiling, bubbling in their belly.

"Morgan, you okay?" Carmen went to put a hand on their shoulder, then thought better of it. Morgan waved her away, shut their eyes and took one last deep breath, really tucking it into every corner of their lungs before letting it out in a huge rush. It was far too soon to face up to old memories again, far too soon. They left the others to fuss over Susan and ran into the semi-tamed wilderness of the cemetery proper.

The headstones and statues were a jumble, the slow movement of the earth pushing up some plots, dipping others, making it look as if the deceased had crawled out. That the grassy alleys between the plots needed cutting meant that Morgan, lying down on the slab of a forgotten relative, was hidden from the chapel and shed. With arms outstretched, staring straight up at the sky low with clouds, Morgan wrinkled their mouth and let the memories wash over them. Not complete memories, sometimes just impressions of emotions or smells but memories all the same. Over all of it, a shroud of agony. Panic and dread clutched at their heart, shortened their breath. They curled onto their side and bit down on their fist hard, screaming into it, in fear and shame.

"Susan, I really think we should be getting you medical assistance. You've gone awfully pale." Natasha was clutching an unwanted mug of tea, courtesy of George, between her hands to stop the shaking. She was sat by the shed door, swaying side to side.

"Pale is just part of my look and I've already told you my mates will come back for me. We're family, yeah?" Susan sighed and shut her eyes against the hot pain.

"Susan, did your friends steal our tools?"

"Yeah."

"Oh. Okay."

"Why you lot still here anyhow? You get paid for it? Hoping to rebuild the economy or summit?"

"Force of habit, I suppose. Money was never anything to write home about even before everything changed. It was nice to feel a part of something, to have the experience." Natasha frowned into her rapidly cooling tea before draining it off and placing the mug aside, clasping her worn hands together and examining the callouses. Susan shifted her weight, trying to alleviate the agony in her side but the movement made it worse and she bit down on a moan. She was feeling light-headed and nauseous, was finding it hard to stay awake. She drifted into a doze, only to witness exploding lights as Natasha slapped her, hard.

"Stay awake!"

I am going to watch this woman bleed out all over the shed floor and I don't think I will cope, she thought and screwed up her face against tears of panic. She let out a long breath and nodded as she made up her mind.

"I'm phoning an ambulance. No, shut up! I'm not going to watch you die. Besides, friends wouldn't stab a friend and leave them to die alone." Natasha took off her work cap and jammed it onto Susan's head.

"Now you're one of us so fucking well act like it." Natasha marched out of the shed and took a deep breath to calm herself. Her legs were foal-new as she staggered towards the chapel and the only working phone on site.

Morgan wiped their eyes with a ragged tissue found in their trouser pocket and sat up. The sky was white from horizon to horizon, a chill breeze picking up. Pulling their jacket tighter around their body, they stood up and frowned down at the shed under its hawthorn tree. The conflict within Morgan boiled over and they vomited into the grass, a hacking, suffocating sensation that burned the back of their throat. A moan slipped out between their lips, their entire body a roiling mess. They took deep breaths and waited for a fragile calm to settle over them before stalking back down between the headstones, towards the chapel where Natasha had disappeared.

She was on the phone, twirling the looped cord between thumb and forefinger as it rang and rang.

~Everything okay?~ Morgan frowned.

"Just phoning an ambulance for Susan."

Morgan tore the phone from Natasha's grip and slammed it onto the desk.

~Do you know what she did to me? Look!~ Morgan opened her mouth wide, stretched their jaw until it creaked with the strain. Natasha's eyes bulged out of her head as she stared at the shriveled stump that had once been a working muscle.

"Morgan, I cannot imagine what that was like and I'm too much of a coward to ask but we can't let Susan bleed out all over the shed floor. The

13

police will ask too many questions." She flinched as Morgan swept the old leaflets and change tray to the floor, upended the table and smashed it to the flagstone floor. The crash echoed throughout the chapel, startling pigeons from the rafters. She stepped back one step, two.

"Morgan, please, she doesn't deserve to die."

Morgan barked a laugh, jarring against Natasha's ears. They began to sign very slowly, each movement clipped and precise.

~I would have thought you, of all people, would have understood having something taken from you, to have something stolen.~

"The tools are repla-"

~I'm not talking about the fucking tools. Pride, I'm talking about your pride and self-worth. She made me beg and, and-~ They stopped, balled their hands into fists at their sides.

"Morgan?" Natasha reached a hand out and placed it on their arm. "Morgan, we can't just leave her to die. If we do, we're no better than them." Morgan's breathing deepened and they stared straight ahead, motionless.

And then a flurry, a whirlwind of arms and fists as they struck Natasha around the face and she crumpled to the ground. Morgan closed the chapel door quietly behind them, under the eyes of the ruffled pigeons and began to lope back to the shed. All they could see, all that they could feel was the blade at the corner of their mouth, the slow-sharp memory of pain and the hot stream of piss as it ran down their leg.

There was no way the team could understand those captive weeks or the pain and humiliation. Nobody but Susan.

George and Carmen popped their heads into the chapel. They were ruffled and crowned with burrs and leaves, but wore smiles.

"We found the tools!" Carmen held out a spade, jiggling the rakes and hoes in the crook of her arm. Her glasses were fogged up from the exertion. George placed the secateurs on the table as if he were handling an angry snake.

"How's our patient?" he asked.

"Morgan's with her. I'd come to ring an ambulance, but I don't think they'll be coming. Let me help you with those."

The three trooped out of the chapel, leaving the door ajar. The only valuable thing left was George's stash of tea and biscuits. Natasha breathed in deep, started to drag behind the other two as they came closer to the shed. Stepping into the shade of the hawthorn tree, a shudder ran through her and she clutched the bundle of rakes and spades closer to her chest.

"Morgan! We found our tools!" Carmen skipped the last steps towards the shed door. Morgan emerged, her bottom lip tucked under their teeth.

"Is she okay?" Carmen dropped the tools in a clatter onto the ground. Morgan shook their head, folded their hands. Carmen and George piled into the shed, shouting, crying, checking for a pulse. Morgan met Natasha's eye. She lowered her bundle to the ground as if it were the most precious thing in the world.

~I know what you've done.~ Natasha's hands were small, skittish rabbits sprinting away from fox jaws. Morgan's hands hung silent by their sides.

Cogs

Going through the procedure is supposedly an honour and privilege. It is the highest level of recognition of my everyday ability, knowledge and skill at my job.

Mate, I just come in, do my job and go home. Everyone here does that too - just sometimes - well, every day, I pump out more work than my team combined and make far fewer mistakes. Now this procedure has marked me out as management's pet when all I wanted was a job to pay the rent at the end of the month.

There have already been two people go through the process - the selection is every six months (around performance review time). There's no asking, no debate or application, you just get a letter all fancy-like, congratulations all round - pat management on the back. Joy. I mean, my team like me, I think, and they joke about my being a machine, sometimes are in awe at how much I can process in a day alone but sometimes I catch a glimpse of something like envy in their faces, a tightening of a frown, an impatient word, and it does make me wonder if I'm as popular as management say I am.

It's 7:00am on Monday morning, thundering down with rain and my yellow slicker is stuck to my skin. The foyer is empty but for security lounging about at the on-site coffee bar. Quiet murmurs with the bar staff, the THUD THUD of the coffee tamp being emptied. The hiss and squeal of the machine as it froths the milk, the click click of the jug and finally, ah - coffee. I wipe my feet on the matt and swipe my pass in, first at the door, then through the security gate. The conversation continues at the coffee bar with no indication of hello. They know where I'm going. Take the lift down to the basement - gym with a solitary runner, the door to the carpark, and the security door at the other end of the corridor, dark blue printed with AUTHORISED PERSONNEL ONLY.

Strictly, I shouldn't be here - security concerns, industrial espionage and all that. As if I would do that. And besides management said it was okay - had my entry pass upgraded and everything.

Which I swipe down the lock now, submit my thumb print and breathe out at the THUNK of the lock. The door clicks shut behind me, I lean against it just for a moment and catch my breath. I hadn't noticed I'd been holding it.

"Good morning, Joe. How was your weekend?" A blue table in the centre of the room, with three pairs of people, three sets of twins, settled amongst coffee and toast. I smile at my mirror image.

"Quiet, thank you. I finished my book." I pull up a chair, pour a cup of coffee from the pot. I am adrift in an ocean of twins and it is still unnerving six months on from the procedure.

I come down to this white-washed cool-room every single morning, share a cup of coffee and chit-chat with the residents. I'm still not entirely sure *why* though. After this morning ritual, we head on upstairs to our desks together - because we are a team after all. A duplicated, quiet team of identical machines. Spot the difference.

The morning of my procedure was cold and blustery, and I couldn't seem to wrap up in enough layers, couldn't tame the raging anxiety flooding my system. There's only so much blurb you can read regarding such an operation - less operation and more going for a long luxurious nap - but knowing what would be happening around you, to you, while you were pretending to be dead was still terrifying.

I stood at the window of the high-rise hotel, watching the dawn traffic scuttle around below. No expense spared, a massage before lunch, a hearty five-course dinner served by crisply pressed waiters with white gloves. Now it's crunch time. A polite knock at my door, a polite smile, a polite, "Good morning, Joe. Did you sleep well?"

"I guess," is my perhaps too-blunt, too-honest reply. Management would have picked me up on that. That's not very Company Tone, is it? Not too positive or concrete. What could you have said instead?

But management weren't there - I was alone and chaperoned by strangers who had probably never heard of us in the first place. For all the bigging up for this honour, this privilege, management only went so far.

The clinic was a squat building set back from the road, sitting amongst prime, neat grounds. A frosted glass panel out the front claimed this was Lab Inc - *Boosting Productivity since 2015!* Only the glitz and glamour were really mute and dull in the dawn rain. Their reception was supposed to be a cool, neutral blue but it came off as cold and distant. The place was populated by a single, sleepy receptionist covering her yawn with a clawed hand. Her scarlet nail polish was like a flare in the gloom.

"Good morning. Could I take your name please?" She shuffled the mouse, tapped something on her keyboard.

"Joe," I said.

"I'll let Dr Patel know you're here. Can I get you a glass of water?"

"Er - no, thanks." I retreated, sat down and took out my book. I had only twenty pages remaining and was forced to read really slowly if I wanted something to do on the train home.

Thankfully, Dr. Patel was prompt. She was bright and cheerful. She took me through to a little room, all pastels and box folders.

And then everything goes a little quicker, my memory of getting into a gown, climbing into a very crisp, very clean bed. A nurse setting up a drip - what was the drip for?! - and all smiles and manners and, "A little scratch. There, now if you'll just count backwards from ten."

Ten, nine, eight –

Mondays are always busy in the energy industry for back room personnel. All of the queries that were unanswerable over the weekend have piled up and the phone is off the hook, and you find yourself repeating a lot of the same things and - I already spoke to you about this account.

However, when you're pegged as an asset, you get moved into the older pots of work - the accounts where other agents have no clue what needs to happen to get it updated and a statement produced.

New week, new pot of work. I smile at Blake because he's on the phone this morning and we all know his feelings about that. His patience is saint-like with the call centre operatives. He gives a little dip of his head, arranging his glass of water and mug of coffee within arm's reach.

My twins still unnerve him, I see. A tight smile, hunched shoulders. It's not to everyone's taste - we had one team member go AWOL when they discovered I was going in for the procedure.

"It's unnatural!" she had screamed and then walked out. She left her computer on and never came back.

"Joe, which pot of work do you want to tackle first?"

"I'll have the NAP pot, please."

"Very well, I'll take the main pot and B will work the System pot." A gives me a wide grin, typing without looking at their screen. Their teeth are shiny, straight and white - a little upgrade when they were being grown. I have teeth stained yellow from too much coffee. It does make me wonder what else they've changed about them. Are they still attracted to men? Or did they take out desire, the ability to love?

Looking at my twins (no, not *mine* even though they came from me), it feels like I am being slowly replaced: they don't get sick. Ever. If I should leave the company, they'll stay on. They will work here until they die. Can they die? The only death of a twin ever broadcast in the news that I could find was a suicide but aside from that, we have never been shown a natural death of a twin. There are some pages buried deep in the internet stating that twins will be just recreated if they die - that my DNA will be kept on file forever and ever, amen.

Imagine a tiny part of you going on and on for who knows how long doing the same work day in, day out. No holidays, maybe no retirement even - will they just die from exhaustion?

And sometimes when I'm half awake at 3am, blinking at my alarm clock, listening to my neighbours argue for the millionth time that week, I wonder. Wonder what'll happen if I always perform 100% - will people start mistaking me for a copy. Mistake me for a man-made machine.

A Brother's Love

Andrew loved his baby brother dearly, like his heart would explode, but right now he could throttle him.

He'd been sat with his slowly coagulating Cappuccino for an hour now and the damn thing had cost nearly £2.50. He turned the page of the newspaper that he'd half read three times now, executing the shuffle shuffle-flick maneuver with newly-found ease. And just as he was considering phoning his baby brother, Mark came loping around the corner, a little sweaty, a little crumpled. Mark collapsed into the wicker chair opposite his half-brother, only a little out of breath.

"Sorry, sorry, I-" he began to pant for breath, Andrew raising a cool eyebrow.

"And what time do you call this?" he tapped his watch, a bootleg from the flea market.

"I ran into Sam on the way over and we just got talking." Mark blushed and it spread to the tips of his ears until he was a spitting image of a midsummer sunset. Andrew quirked a grin and chugged the last of his cold, greasy Cappuccino, getting up with the silky grace inherited from his mother.

"When do I get to meet her then?" He clapped his brother around the shoulders, "have you kissed her yet?" He began to steer Mark around the corner, where the food market spread out before them in a cacophony of fragrant steam, smoky barbeque and bright, gem-like cakes. The stalls were arranged in a ring around the outskirts of the square and, although the lunchtime buzz had died down, there were still a few queues snaking through the space.

Mark stopped short, bit his lip.

"Andy, listen, I-"

"Look, you're not still doubting this, doubting me? Come on, bro, we've been through this already."

"No, it's not this, it's-" Mark took a breath and hissed it out his nose, "Sam's a bloke. I'm bisexual, Andy."

Andrew blinked at his baby brother, mind blank. Mark looked at his feet, face now well and truly looking like he'd been roasted by the sun, his freckles near-gone.

"I don't know what that means."

"Forget it, let's get this over with." Mark didn't so much stomp away, but was a brewing storm, hands in his pockets, head bowed into the aromatic steam swirling over the market. He approached the Italian street food vendor, a bright pitch of red, white and green serving fresh pasta with tomato sauce, pesto or roasted vegetables, meatballs. The server was a large white woman wearing a white apron flicked with dried tomato sauce, her curly, bouncy hair tamed under a handkerchief.

Andrew caught up with his brother, slapped an arm around his shoulders and so the game began.

"This is the place I was telling you about, bro. And I already checked with Sarah here and you're okay! No celery here! Have whatever takes your fancy, I'll treat you."

The pair picked the pasta and meatballs in tomato sauce (with a kick of chili). Andrew was salivating like a dog at the smell and forgot for a beat what he was really here for.

It all came back with his baby brother taking the first bite of his meal, and his dairy allergy kicked in. Mark had perfected the fall to his knees as his stomach rebelled and his body began to reject his meal. Andrew played his part of concerned big brother perfectly, fumbling his phone from his pocket, shaking, shouting for a paramedic - anybody - to help.

And it was supposed to go like this:

1. Ambulance was called.

2. Mark is bundled into the back.

3. Andrew takes details of the food vendor to follow up later.

4. Mark recovers in A&E, to laugh about it all later.

5. They write to the vendor to sue for damages.

6. Money comes pouring in, nice dinners all round.

Only, something had gone wrong. Mark was curled into himself, whimpering like a kicked dog, sweating, pale. He'd never gone down so heavy before, been reduced to such a state. His eyes sought Andrew, who knelt beside his brother.

"Andy, this wasn't part of the plan," Mark whispered.

"I know, Mark. Just hold on and we'll get you to the hospital."

The ambulance took forty minutes to arrive, in which time Mark had fallen unconscious and a small crowd had gathered around them. Somebody had put Mark into the recovery position, but Andrew had forgotten to thank them, to even acknowledge them. The paramedics had bundled Mark onto a gurney and Andrew had left with them, forgetting to take the name of the Italian food vendor to follow up. All the way to the hospital Andrew squeezed Mark's hand and whispered to him.

Andrew's last sight of his baby brother was his unconscious form being wheeled into the bowels of the hospital, flanked by an army of blue-scrubbed staff. He collapsed into a flat seat in the waiting room, surrounded by injured humanity, staring at his shoes. This wasn't part of the plan. He still didn't know what to do with his hands so to stop them moving he tucked them into his armpits, only then his legs starting twitching. It didn't matter in the end. A nurse in blue scrubs approached Andrew, sat down beside him and confirmed what he already knew in his soul: Mark was gone.

Andrew somehow managed to get home, running on autopilot when locking the front door, putting his keys in the dish, coat on hook. He sat on their tiny, sagging sofa and stared at the carpet. It hadn't quite sunk in yet, but the numb in his heart was spreading. He had to tell people, tell their mum, tell that bloke, Sam.

Andrew didn't know Sam. It'd sounded like Mark was pretty into him, but wasn't gay?

The thin twilight was smothered by the night, their small matchbox of a living room illuminated by the sodium orange streetlight. Andrew was jolted out of his circling darkness by the ring of the landline. He stared at the pale blue of the screen with a mobile number he didn't recognise, let it ring three times before picking it up.

"Hello?" he choked.

"Hello? Mark? It's Sam."

"Oh, Mark isn't here. He—"

"You must be Andy! Mark's told me so much about you."

"Really? He mentioned you today, before he— I—" Andrew's core broke and the sobs bubbled up out of him.

"Has something happened? Are you okay?"

"No," Andrew whispered.

"I'm coming over. Just hold tight, Andy."

Sam arrived in his dented, tiny Vauxhall Opel Corsa and managed to find a gap on the street. The porchlight highlighted Sam's high cheekbones, his long, pale lashes and the galaxy of freckles across his nose. He was absolutely gorgeous.

"I bought tea and milk," Sam said as way of an introduction, holding up a plastic Budgens carrier bag.

"Please come in." Andrew invited Sam into the tiny nook of a kitchen, with its colour scheme out of the Sixties. He found some clean, chipped mugs and managed to fill the kettle, even with his shaking, numb hands.

"Let me, Andy. Sugar?" Sam gave him a small smile, settled into the ritual of making tea. They settled on the sofa, the room a little chilly, lit by a single fourty-watt bulb. They blew on their tea, small curls of vapour twisting up to kiss their noses.

Just who was this helpful stranger? Coming round to make tea and listen to somebody else's woes? Andrew peeked out the corner of his eyes, taking in Sam's profile, his petit nose and brush of freckles.

"Mark's dead." The words were a quiet hiss of admission, the grief starting to bleed through and crush his chest.

"I spoke to him, saw him this afternoon." Sam cradled his mug, staring at Andrew from under his long lashes.

"We met up afterwards and tried the food market and he… he died alone in the hospital. I wasn't in the room with him." Andrew bit into his fist, turning away as the sobs shook his body. Mark had died alone because of him, because of his stupid get-rich-quick scheme. Could he tell Sam about that? Should he?

Andrew placed his mug on the low table, covering his face with his hands as his grief and guilt poured out. Sam was crying too, but in a quiet, snuffling-type of way. He curled his arm about Andrew's shoulder and it was like an electric shock. Andrew was on his feet, pedaling to the other side of the room.

"Don't touch me! I don't want whatever it is you've caught!"

"Sorry, Andy, what have I caught?"

"You're gay, aren't you? Don't you all have AIDs?" Sam took a breath, wiped his eyes with his fingers.

"Yes, I am gay. No, I don't have AIDs, tested negative for HIV as it happens. Look, Andy, I didn't come over here to put up with homophobic bullshit. I came because you sounded distraught on the phone and I know Mark cared for you a great deal."

"I didn't know Mark was gay. He never told me."

"He wasn't gay. Mark was bisexual. He was attracted to men and women."

"But he was seeing you?"

Sam let out a small sigh and took a gulp of tea. He hadn't expected to be giving a lesson in sexuality to his dead to-be partner's older half-brother.

"Mark was bisexual, even though he was in a same-sex relationship. You don't just stop being bisexual when you're dating someone of the same sex."

Andrew took a moment to chew over this explanation.

"So, Mark was dating a man and a woman?"

"I don't think Mark was polyamorous, so no. Listen, Andy, if there's anything you need, give me a ring." He took pen and paper from his coat pocket, wrote down his number and placed it on the table, stood up and brushed his trousers down. "Please let me know when the funeral is. I'd like to say goodbye." Sam cleared his throat and left, closing the front door behind him. Andrew listened to the growl of the car fade into the distance, looking at the small rectangle of paper on the table. It was only when he was clearing away the half-drunk tea that he noticed Sam had left the milk behind.

Settlement 16

There were good perks in being the only policeman in Settlement 16, like having a non-shared house, with space and quiet lulls in the day. But it did mean business hours didn't apply. Or, even worse, in Thomas' opinion, it meant that people would just drop by at all hours, and only to shoot the breeze.

Thomas had removed his side arm holster, hung it on its hook by the door and was beginning to wind down. This involved the day's highlight: removing his binder. It began with unbuttoning his work shirt and hanging it up to serve tomorrow's stint at the station, as there wasn't enough water to have a clean shirt every weekday. And then the absolute pleasure of removing his binder and breathing into his lungs, expanding his chest cavity completely.

Only tonight, a Wednesday (not that it really mattered because this job was seven days a week), Thomas was already heating beans on the camping stove, in his tatty dressing gown, when the knock came. It was not a desperate hammering or a timid patter, but a cheery pattern that Thomas knew all too well: somebody wanted a chat. He sighed, lowered the heat under his beans and pulled his dressing gown close, tied it tight and prepared to have a chat.

"Good evening, Mr Baker. What seems to be the trouble?" Kevin Baker was on the settlement council and breezed through his days ignoring the citizens with ideas that he didn't agree with, and stealing other people's work. With his short, blonde hair and button-down, pressed shirt, he made Thomas' teeth itch. He was sure Baker was siphoning water, but Thomas had no evidence.

"Tom! Just the, er, man I need. Can I come in a spell?"Thomas opened the door wider and invited the councilman into his sanctuary. He needed to set up an audience room, just a small space to keep business calls and his down-time separate.

Kevin claimed the only chair in Thomas' house, perched on the very edge and smiled up at Thomas.

"I see you're about to have dinner so I'll keep it short. Tom, people are nervous, and the impression is that the police department aren't taking them seriously."

"Sorry councilman, but you've lost me." Thomas leant against the kitchen counter, resigned to a late dinner.

"There's an outsider. He comes and goes, stands and watches. Lucy has seen him every day this week in her croplands. Nobody knows how he gets in and out." Kevin leaned back in the chair, took Thomas' binder and drew his eyebrows together. He held it up.

"It's a binder, Mr Baker. People aplenty wear them."

"Thomas, you don't have to keep disguising your body as a man: the people know you're a tip-top policeman and your being a woman has nothing to do with it."

"With all due respect councilman-"

"Please, Tom, that's a later conversation, but right now I need you to investigate this outsider and see what he wants, okay? And should it be necessary, arrest him."

"Very well, Mr Baker, I'll get on that tomorrow."

"Excellent! The people will sleep easy knowing you're on the case." Kevin got up and pinched his sharp trouser lines into place, shook Thomas' hand and was gone. Thomas locked the door and rested his head against it, shutting his eyes. He took a deep breath in and whispered, "you little weasel."

Dawn wasn't a glorious sunrise, the sky a piece of yellow layer cake morphing through to blue, no. The haze just lightened a little and settled on eggshell white most days. The only blue skies they got anymore were when the solar winds crashed into the atmosphere, but that's when the sun would be too hot to handle and people would stay inside lest they develop the sun-sickness.

But that season was still months away, so Thomas rose with the haze-change, ate a cold meal (overnight oats, seeds and a precious yoghurt dollop on top) and got into yesterday's clothes. They didn't smell so bad, but he'd have to sort out a washing ration sooner rather than later.

The settlement was still quiet, only Thomas and a growing group heading out to the croplands, greenhouse and polytunnels. He nodded to the only other living souls on his way to work and took a deep breath to mark the new work day, and a new investigation.

But as tranquil as the day had begun, that went out the window as Thomas came up to the police station, a small two-storey glass and chrome building, and he saw that councilman Baker had already spoken to those people who had seen the outside. They were a crowd twenty-strong, and Thomas knew most by name, some by sight. He put on a small, welcoming smile and climbed the short ramp leading up to the entrance. The people all began talking at once and Thomas held out his hands to quieten them.

"I understand there have been sightings, an outside who has made his way into the settlement and you are concerned by his motives. I am, today, opening a new case to determine his intentions and to take the next steps, should they be needed, to keep Settlement 16 in check. But to do this, I need to speak to you one at a time, on record, to stay within the law. So, please make your way into reception and I will call you through when I'm set up, okay? Thank you. Your patience and assistance are appreciated."

Thomas opened up the station and let the citizens take over the reception area and the brittle plastic scoop chairs in small groups. Somebody had been generous enough to spare precious ingredients to bake a lemon drizzle cake to share, and everybody had a tea canteen. Thomas cleared his desk in interview room two (room one had been turned into a dry goods store) so the interviews might stay on track better. He took another deep breath, this one to acknowledge how patient he was right now, and then called in Lucy Williams to begin.

Lucy wheeled into Thomas' interview room with a burlap sack on her lap. She was a black woman in her mid-thirties, a wheelchair user since her teens, and the croplands overseer. She wore no-nonsense blouses and dungarees with sturdy boots. They had known each other since they had learnt to read and Lucy had been there when Thomas had chosen his new name.

Lucy placed the sack on the desk, grinning.

"New strawberries, but don't tell anybody, yeah?" She winked and settled her hands in her lap, all business now. Thomas allowed a small moment to select a strawberry, ruby-red and only a little bigger than his thumb nail, and pop it in his mouth. Lucy let him have a moment to luxuriate in the sweet-blooming across his tongue.

"Thank you, Lucy. Now, tell me everything you think you know about this outsider."

"I noticed him two weeks ago, in the north-western cropland and each day he moved over one cropland, closer to the settlement. He is average height, almost skeleton-thin. He wore the same clothes, trouser, shirt and baseball cap, so I didn't get any nitty details. Thomas, I know he's making people nervous, but he's just watching. This guy does nothing, doesn't even wave or smile. I don't think he's dangerous, maybe just lonely? I know that's pure speculation, but I think he would have done something by now." Thomas scribbled everything down, nodding encouragement. There was a reason he was speaking to Lucy as his opening witness and that's because she took the time to think things through.

"He didn't speak to you?"

"No, nothing like that. I didn't even attempt to approach him: harvest is nearly upon us. But I think he will be in the south-east cropland today, should he keep to the pattern." She knocked on the tabletop with another grin.

"I knew you'd have something good. What time does he usually appear?"

"Thumbs breath preceding noon." Thomas underlined his notes with a long line and nodded.

"I'm going to need Luke. Will you indulge me and deliver him here? I'm going to see about having a chat with this outsider."

With Lucy's statement delivered and with a little time spare while Luke came down to the station in his capacity as assistant, Thomas called in the next witness. He was scribbling down their name when shouting broke the relative calm in the reception. Thomas bid the witness wait while he sorted out the disturbance and poked his head about the door.

Standing in the reception, beet-red and chest heaving, wearing crumpled clothes, was Carl. Carl was Settlement 16's original resident, knew it when it had been little more than a tent-city. He knew the place better than anybody. He had dragged in May Stimple, a child no more than nine summers whose whole body was shaking under Carl's grip.

"Tom! You've got to do something about these brats" I caught this one taking a shit in the lake. That's our water source. I don't want to be drinking some kid's shit!" He shook May, but she didn't cry out, only struggled to loosen his vice-grip.

"Calm down, Carl. Let the girl go." Thomas held up his hands and took a couple of steps into reception. "I understand your point, I do, but terrorising the children isn't going to solve this." All eyes were on him, and a mumbling hush settled over reception. To Carl's credit, he did release May's arm and she ran over to Tom, hiding behind him.

"The crystal system isn't designed to deal with anything more than duck shit, Tom. The water source gets polluted and we won't last."

"Okay, Carl, I'll tell you what I propose to do. I'll speak to May and her dad and we'll set up something with the teachers, get them to explain to the kids why the lake isn't a playground or a toilet. We'll sort this."

"See that you do, Thomas. I won't have our water supply taken away. I remember what it was like when we had to rely on boiling rain water and tablets. And I say, never again." Carl stormed out, the doors crashing open and shut. Thomas whistled, shaking his head at the outburst but, truly, he understood Carl's argument: where do you draw the line with little misdemeanours?

He took May's hand and escorted her out the building. His assistant Luke was sprinting down the road and Thomas gave him instructions to take as many statements as possible about the outsider. He was taking May home to speak to her dad, and then would attempt to catch the outsider in the south-east cropland, "attempt" being the operative word.

May's dad was a single parent and his little girl was everything to him since losing his partner. He was embarrassed at her actions and swore he would give May a big talking to. He was also pretty cute when he blushed.

"Just make sure she understands she isn't in trouble, but this is important. There are other places to use as a toilet." Thomas shook Max's hand and gave May a smile and a wink. He just hoped this would be the only incident, otherwise he might have to step in properly.

With a last wave at the house, Thomas began the short trek to Settlement 16's walls. The place was built in a large grid, with the people and buildings inside the stockade. Outside the walls lay Lucy's immaculate croplands on three sides and the lake sweeping around in a curve, an untidy horseshoe shape. Thomas climbed the ladder to the ramparts and began a slow walk around the top, nodding to the lookouts in passing. The haze was illuminated by the small sun, a cloudy yellow disk that was nearing its zenith, and a breeze was picking up, bringing with it the singing and industry-noise in the croplands. Thomas took in the outside view and then threw a rope ladder over the side to get into the south-east cropland.

The very edge was a vast greenhouse row, busy with people potting seedlings ready to be transplanted into the croplands' soil. There were onions, peppers, carrots and broccoli, bean and pea tripods. Some labourers waved at Thomas through the glass, and he smiled and nodded back, making his way across the boards set down as a path between planting sections. He stepped onto the dry earth, already marked out with string and stakes depending on which crop was destined to take up residence, dodging and weaving around the groundwork until he was in the dead centre. It was quiet and there was a glimmer in the distance to mark the lake, where the land dipped into a natural depression. Thomas marked the time by the haze-disc and was relieved he was a little early, that maybe he would spot the outsider's approach. But he'd been distracted by the lake-shimmer and it was only when somebody stepped up beside him that he realised he wasn't alone. He startled, took a step back and let his heart calm a little. He hadn't planned on what he was going to say, but the outsider beat him to it.

"My name is Edith Smith and I am here to warn you. I know my presence over the last two weeks has been suspicious, but you are in great danger. Your walls will not be enough to save you and you will be absorbed into the insatiable thirst that is coming your way."

"Wait, hold on a minute. Edith, yeah? I'm Thomas Spencer, policeman, and concerns have been raised about your appearances around here. I have some questions I'd like answers to, as I'm sure the people would like too. So, let me ask you this: why are you here?" Thomas managed to get a glimpse under Edith's hat and wished he hadn't because her neck and head were puckered with livid scar tissue.

"The Raiding Queen has consolidated all the bands in the west, brought them under her banner, and now she sweeps through the land, absorbing all. My people were given a choice, join her or die. We declined, because it was our land, our right to live under our own rule. She came in the night-death and put our homes to the torch, captured everybody and started to make examples to show the whole land what happens when you deny her will. I was lucky." Edith looked Thomas dead in the eye, tilted her head back to show him she spoke the truth. It turned his stomach, so he shut his eyes.

"How long do we have?"

"Six weeks, but I have some ideas. Let me help you."

"Why are you doing this?"

"Because nobody should go through what I did: things are hard enough as they are without being threatened and tortured. I can't let it happen again." Thomas mulled her words over a moment and decided it was too big a risk to not believe her - but he certainly didn't trust her.

"Okay, you'll need to speak with the council, they're the decision makers, but go easy: we don't need a panic."

"I think a panic will be inevitable."

The council chambers were the beating heart that made up Settlement 16, and sat at the centre. It was a large enough building to hold every citizen at a rare emergency meeting. Thomas escorted Edith up the back stairs, wooden and creaky, to avoid as many people as possible, at least until the council had made a decision regarding Edith's plan. He knocked on the council chambers doors and waited, knocked again when there was no answer and decided that this couldn't wait and opened the door, to councilman Baker's annoyance. He had been mid-sentence, and he glowered at Thomas.

"What is this, Thomas? Didn't I give you a job to do?"

"Yes, you did, and here's your outsider. Her name is Edith and she has a message, a warning and I think we need to listen to her."

"Yes, you must listen. Your town is in danger, a raiding party is heading this way and you are not in a position to hold out. She goes by the name Bandit Queen and she will show you no quarter."

"And what evidence do you have?" Baker demanded, still standing behind his desk. Edith removed her hat and tilted her head back so they could see everything, the lips and eyelids hacked away, sick skin blossoming with grey patches, pink shiny burns and the creeping bruised scars that attracted and held the eye.

"Saints alive, she did this?" Baker's countenance drained, something Thomas had never witnessed.

"With her own hand. Now, listen to me. I think I can help you save your people but we have to act now."

The council, seven elected everyday people, looked at each other, panicked.

"Thomas, when I'd said to investigate, I didn't mean bring doom on us," Kevin whispered.

"Noted, councilman. I'll send the signal; gather the people and we can make a start." Thomas straightened his sidearm holster and marched out; hands clenched to stop them shaking.

The signal included lighting a beacon on the town hall's spire and clanging the bell in the steeple. The noise echoed back, reverberated through the surrounding buildings and caused a great stirring in the streets and croplands. Jobs were abandoned and the people crushed together to get up the town halls steps, to gather in the meeting hall, a muttering, roiling body nervous.

Edith caused a stir when invited onto stage, and there poured anguish and anger as she told her story and outlined her plan. And then complete silence, eerie and haunting as though they had already been slaughtered. The plan was outlandish and dangerous - it had to work otherwise they would be destroyed, but it meant digging up great swathes in the croplands, greatly reducing the harvest later on in the year. The croplands would be lain with great spike traps, pitch traps to be set alight, and huge pits to be dug, deeper than any one man could climb out, unaided.

"And should they get through all that?" Lucy was at the crowd centre, holding her hand up.

"Then you will need to prepare yourselves, but I know that a demonstration like this will be enough to drive her away." Edith held her hands up to placate the crowd, begging them to listen, to believe her. Lucy caught Thomas' eye and he nodded very slightly. Trust me.

"Very well, I don't like it - those croplands took time to prepare - but I volunteer to arrange this upheaval. All my work…" She trailed into silence, shook her head. "Cropland lottery, with me."

The crowd parted as Lucy wheeled away, out the hall, and she was accompanied by the cropland growers, a good third in the hall. With the populace thinned - nobody had ever thought about just how many people were needed to grow their crops - a slight panic spark was threatening to kindle.

"Settlement 16, you will remain quiet," Thomas boomed. The panic was eating into his head, making him sweat and nausea rose in his belly. Yesterday had been marked by councilman Baker's transphobic comments and today all that had changed - everything had changed. He nodded at Edith to continue and she took centre stage again. Thomas hadn't noticed previously that she clasped her hands behind her back to stop them shaking. Terror at the events to come? Or terror when speaking to so many people?

"I have observed your walls, and I believe they can be adapted, that trenches should be dug at the base developed to splash back murder hole pitch, the same should be done against the gate too." Not a small task, but the citizens were coming round to the idea that their very lives were in danger: this was real. Several groups volunteered to start the grueling work involved with trench digging. Panic tinged with excitement was spreading throughout the hall.

"The rest, we have the most important task, the task that'll ensure your survival: stockpiling supplies, water and rations, stock-taking weapons and anything else paramount to survival. And I think your policeman would be best suited." Edith gave him a small smile and nodded. Thomas stepped to the stage centre and took a breath. This was all a bad dream.

"Right, right, I propose the remnant split

into six and elect a spokesperson, you will report directly to me. Decide which teams want to haul and stockpile water, vitals, medical supplies, weapons. The last two teams, you will be on reverse to swap rotas. Once you're ready, spokespeople to me." The hall buzzed like a wasp's nest as the people organised themselves.

"Edith, we're not the only town you've helped, are we?" Thomas caught her eye and she shook her head very slightly. "What happened to the rest?"

"They either chased me away, laughed at me or decided to give in. Nobody has taken a stand until now."

"I just hope this works. Otherwise this'll do more harm than good."

"I believe in you, Thomas. Truly, I do."

Frantic

Sophia was hauled awake by the frozen submersion of her face, neck and shoulders. Her eyes snapped open, blurry and stinging. She was sprawled on a chilled grille floor, dressed in a grubby grey vest and shorts soaked through. Her feet were bare and going purple with cold. She remembered to breathe and her breath plumed out of her mouth. Her entire emaciated body began to shake.

She managed to climb to her feet, wrapped her arms about her to try and trap what little warmth there was left under her skin. She was in a bleak, metal room with strip lighting and hydraulic doors. There was a hissing, crashing noise and what may have been shouting, screaming. She wringed suspension fluid out of her hair and stumbled up to the bulkhead. It whispered open and somebody grabbed hold of her, wrenched her into a corridor of more bleak grey grilles.

"Dépêchez-vous!" The guard, shielded behind an opaque visor and scaled uniform, waved a dormant cattle prod in Sophia's face.

"I don't understand!" she cried, holding out her shaking, frozen hands. The guard tutted and flicked the prod on, waved it in her face where the thin line of electricity promised pain. She turned on her heel and stumbled down the corridor where doors were whispering open and people were being marched out by more of the same faceless guards. Sophia gulped in massive breaths, trying to keep calm, trying to remember the last thing that had happened before waking up. Nothing. She stumbled on, falling in line behind a black woman with tiny pinprick scars across the back of her neck.

The corridor opened onto a large, empty hall with the long side looked out into the oblivion of space. Sophia stared into that oblivion, jostled by the other people who were whispering to one another.

"Ça va?" The black woman nodded at Sophia.

"I don't understand."

"No French? Well, that'll be interesting for you."

"Sorry?"

"Nothing to be sorry for, just keep your mouth shut and you'll be fine." The black woman had a French accent, the sort of accent Sophia hadn't heard in a very long time. She stared out the window, kept catching her reflection's eye.

"I'm really lost. Where are we?"

"What's the last thing you remember?"

"Nothing. Only coming round on the floor."

"You must have been on the suspension ship, then. I don't know how to say this, but you're on *Le Republique*, the flagship of His Holiness' Left Hand. English, you're on a French ship." Sophia shut her eyes and rested her forehead on the glass.

The holding hall began to rumble, warning klaxons sounding and the bulkhead was locked down with a clatter and thunk that rattled the chest. A murmur of panic swept the crowd as the rumbling stopped and there was a swaying, almost sea-like movement as the hall detached from the main ship.

"We're on a transport," whispered Sophia.

"If we are lucky, they won't vent us," said her companion with a tightening of her mouth. Sophia had read the rumours about prisoners being vented into space if there was no use for them, but they'd only been rumours and nothing had ever come of any investigations into the claims, only reiterations that it would be considered a war crime.

Sophia held out a hand, introduced herself.

"I go by Chou," replied the woman, shaking hands with a firm grip. "It's cabbage," she added at Sophia's blank look.

"Why cabbage?"

"My better half started calling me Chou one day and it stuck. I just kept using it because it made her smile."

"Where is she?"

"Taken at the blockade of Calais."

"That was six months ago."

"Yes, six months, a week and three days to be exact." Chou frowned out into space.

Sophia looked at her feet and tried to wiggle her purple toes, crouched and took her left foot

- like an ice block - between her hands and tried to get a little warmth back into it.

There was a hiss and crackle from the ceiling and a whine of static. A stream of French babbled from hidden speakers and Chou translated.

"We're being taken to a labour station and may be split up from friends and family so we're encouraged to say goodbye."

"A labour station?" Sophia's heart tripped over itself. The murmuring of the other prisoners grew louder and there was crying, shouting, pleading. Chou, however, was studying Sophia.

"What did you say you did?"

"I don't remember."

"Well, try. You do anything useful? More useful than menial labour and we might get through this alive."

"We? Why, what do you do?"

"That doesn't matter, but I can translate for you."

"And what do you get out of this?"

"Help me find something, anything on mon bijou so I can track her down."

Sophia took a moment to look into Chou's round face, her green eyes, weighed up her limited options and then nodded.

"Fine, we have a deal." They shook hands, took a moment to survey the crowd of huddled people. Sophia patted the pockets of her shorts, pulled out an ident-chip. It was palm-sized, grey with her black and white photograph and her travel details.

"I'm a terraform engineer on the way to Colony Eighty-Three for a twelve-year stint. Also says I'm allergic to peanuts. Good to know. Wait, yes, it's coming back to me. I'm a senior engineer, part of the team who helped adjust Jupiter's chemistry enough to put Mining Platform Hercules into orbit."

"That'll be enough to go on for now. Just stick with me and we'll be okay."

"Chou, I know this will hurt and I'm sorry, but what your bijou's name? If I'm going to help track her down, I need to know."

"Masami Otsuka," Chou whispered, breathed out on the window and traced several characters into the fog. Sophia said nothing, only placed a hand on Chou's shoulder.

The docking procedure with the station was bumpy and threw a lot of the prisoners to the metal floor. As the hiss and rumble of the station seeped through the transport, the warning klaxons screamed again and the whole wall opposite the long window began to retract into the ceiling to reveal a multitude of armed guards hefting cattle prods and batons. Ballistics would not do on a space station. The guards, dressed in grey uniforms piped in red, with pips and epaulettes to denote rank and seniority, began to disperse into the huddled, cowering masses and issued orders in swift French. Sophia felt a creeping nausea rising in her stomach, could almost taste the bile. Goose flesh pricked her arms and legs.

"What are they saying, Chou?" she whispered. The klaxon was beginning to give her a headache.

"They're separating out people based on their ages. Just hang tight. Don't speak unless I ask you a question and follow my lead, okay?" Chou took a moment to check her reflection in the window, patted her cornrows and slicked down an eyebrow. Satisfied, she took a deep breath and squared up against the nearest guard.

"Monsieur, cette femme est une ingénieure britannique en terraformation qui affirme que la ventilation d'oxygène peut être à réparer. Elle dit aussi que si cela continue à ce rythme, la prochaine distribution d'oxygène sera nécessaire six mois plus tôt que prévu." Chou sounded urgent and was doing a lot of pointing at Sophia. The Englishwoman tried to make herself smaller, looked at her feet.

"Et comment le savez-vous?" The guard placed the tip of his baton under Sophia's chin and raised it a little so she would look him in the eye.

"Elle ne vous comprend pas. Elle a remarqué la ventilation en entrant avant que nous nous amarrions."

The guard - he must have been only a little over eighteen - held Sophia's gaze before letting it slip, noted her thin vest and shorts, her bare feet.

"Vous avez de la chance d'avoir une traductrice." He smirked and removed the baton, began to walk away. "Venez. Voyons ce que vous pensez savoir sur le fonctionnement d'une station spatiale."

"We might be in luck. Can you fix a space station?" Chou took Sophia's arm and began to pull her along after the guard.

"I can try," Sophia whispered and then vomited all over her bare feet and the floor. They were split off from the other prisoners, caroled down a siding and into a service lift. As they rattled upwards, Sophia could feel the guard's eyes roaming over her and it sent shudders racking through her body. She felt like vomiting again, the smell rising from her feet burning the back of her throat.

And then the guard traced a line from the nape of her neck down to her buttocks, cupped her. She froze, didn't breathe as her mind whirled, dizzy, not knowing how to react.

"Enlevez vos mains." Chou slapped him away, snarled. The guard placed the tip of his baton against Chou's throat and looked her dead in the eye. He pressed against her windpipe.

"Si jamais tu me dis quoi faire à nouveau, je te jette dans l'espace comme la merde que tu es. Suis-je clair?" He took the baton away a beat before the lift doors shuddered open and barked at them. Sophia took Chou's hand and squeezed it, looking for something to focus on that wasn't her spine afire or the cold vomit between her toes. Chou didn't squeeze back, but she didn't let go either.

Sophia was directed to a vis-cube showing the atmospheric readouts of the station. She glanced about the room, at the tiers of vis-cubes and their non-smiling blue and red uniformed guards. The air was warm, enough to take the chill out of her. The smell of vomit - clinging to her hair and toes - made a few people wrinkle their noses but Sophia was left alone with Chou sat beside her.

"What exactly am I supposed to be doing?" whispered Sophia.

"I made up some crap about oxygen deliveries being pulled forward by six months due to venting."

"No, that isn't crap. There's always leaks to be minimised. How do I make this into English?" Sophia started poking the vis-cube gel interface, found a tiny French flag at the bottom of the display and tapping it, saw that she could change the language.

"Listen, I don't know how much time we have, but stall, okay? I'm going to do some digging." Chou began to dip her fingers into the gel interface of her own vis-cube, flicking between screens quicker than Sophia could keep up. The Englishwoman returned to her own interface, wishing she could have a sip of water. Her head was throbbing, making her queasy. She had never been so uncomfortable in her life. Even taking deep, measured breaths through her nose wasn't helping.

"Merde," Chou hissed and rubbed the back of her neck, at the tiny pinprick scars like constellations.

"Have you found her? Your bijou, I mean."

"Non. The people files are encrypted and need a Level Three security clearance." Chou wiped her fingers on her jumper, chewed her lip in thought.

"What does a Level Three security clearance look like?" Sophia continued looking at columns of figures and readouts.

"That asshole in the lift had a Level Three clearance. We'd need either his thumb or ident and an extra minute with a vis-cube."

"This station is huge; chances are we won't find him again." Sophia prayed this to be true, didn't want to be anywhere near him again and his searching, groping hands.

"He's watching the back of your head by the lift. No, don't look. Listen, we're too open here to try anything now, but we can't just wait for an opportunity. We'll have to make one."

"Please, Chou, I don't know how much more I can take of this."

"Listen to me, English. Do you remember those other innocent people we came in with? They're being processed, they are being stolen away from their families and may never see them again. You are in the best position possible right now, even with that asshole taking advantage in the lift."

Sophia nodded, sucked in a breath and held back the tears forming in her eyes. She was torn between pity for herself and pity for those other people. She'd always lived her life in her tiny, comfortable bubble being told to worry about other people, but not too much because her life mattered too. Only she was starting to realise that she'd stopped caring for other people altogether.

"What's your plan if you find Masami in this database? What are the chances of that?"

"Very small, but I have it on good authority that she came through this French sector and so she'll have left a trace on their system. I find that trace and we escape, you carry on with your journey and I carry on finding mon bijou."

"Fine. Follow my lead."

"What are you planning, English?"

"To throw up on that asshole. Be ready."

Sophia lurched to her feet, slapped a hand over her mouth and toppled-swayed the short distance to the lift. He had clocked her as soon as she'd pushed away from the vis-cube.

"Arrêtez!" he called, raising his baton. The console room was poised, statuesque, watching the Englishwoman pause before the guard.

"Please, I'm going to-" Sophia was quite pleased with herself as the thin bile splashed dead centre onto his pristine tunic. Only it was short lived as the baton connected with the side of her head and her vision flickered. She could feel the cold floor along the length of her body, the smell of boot polish, vomit and blood twisting inside her lungs and Chou shouting. The air erupted from Sophia's lungs as the guard kicked her full in the ribs and something moved that shouldn't have.

The console room was a mass of movement and more shouting. Sophia hoped that if she lay still enough, she would pass into oblivion. Her throbbing head was developing into a migraine and now somebody was grabbing hold of her ankles and wrists, turning her onto her back. Something moved in her side and she cried out, screwing her eyes closed.

"S'il te plaît, laissez-moi aller avec elle. Elle ne parle pas du tout Francais."

"Ces anglais sont si peu éduqués. D'accord, aller avec elle mais je vous surveillerai de près!"

"Bien sûr. Merci Monsieur."

Sophia opened her eyes a crack, was blinded by the ceiling lights but for a moment Chou came into view as the unknown hands lifted the Englishwoman onto a stretcher. Sophia tried to follow the conversation as she was jolted back into the lift, but she couldn't guess what the three of them were saying. Instead, she focused on keeping the asshole's ident tucked into her knickers waistband.

The universe was catching up with Chou; so far she'd been playing up the 'black woman supporting white woman through the real uncomfortable truths of Life' but time was running short for her. She had four hours before she needed to check in.

She now sat on the cold, greasy floor of Processing Hub A's medical bay. Sophia was lifted onto a fraying camp bed, still unconscious, still streaked in cold vomit, sweat and tears. A doctor had examined Sophia in absolute silence, had frowned when examining her side, proclaimed a floating rib, but no internal bleeding. With Chou's help, they had wrapped Sophia's chest in thick bandages for support. But then the doctor had disappeared, muttering something about coming back soon.

Chou didn't quite believe her, watching the chaos of the medical bay. It was short on beds, for one thing, with only the seriously injured given a bed and the rest left to sit on the floor or stand. The staff were all hollow-eyed, exhausted, working in near silence, some looking as if they hadn't had a clean set of clothes for three or four days or enough food. Chou pulled her knees up, under her chin and settled in to watch, counting numbers of people, trying to gauge how many of those brought in on the shuttle had already been examined and were further down processing.

She moved her hands into her long sleeves with as little fuss as possible, still counting, still putting together patterns. With the smallest of clicks, she activated the pictma concealed in the lining of her sleeve and began to tease it away from its cocoon. She tucked it between her fingers and laid her hands flat against her shin, working at looking terrified. She couldn't remember how long its memory was, but the tricky bit would be tucking the pictma back into its cocoon with as little fuss as possible.

Of the three-hundred and nineteen souls taken by *Le Republique*, fifty-two were still here, older people who might still be put to work. Chou was trying to remember how many younger people had been present, but Sophia was stirring. The Englishwoman groaned and put a hand over her eyes, the other reached into the band of her shorts.

"Are we alone?" she muttered.

"Non. But nobody's watching." Sophia pulled out the stolen ident and palmed it off to Chou.

"Very good, English. I didn't think you had it in you. Now we just need to find a suitable terminal and maybe we get lucky." Chou tucked both the ident and pictma into her sleeve and turned her attention back to the maelstrom of the medical bay.

It was a long hall, screened off from both ends by double doors. There were no windows and two long drains ran parallel down the length of the hall. The smell from them almost had a mouth-feel, and the water trickling down them was equal parts blood, sweat and urine. There were chrome-brushed sinks every few feet or so, but most of the taps didn't seem to be working.

And there, nestled by the out-door like a quiet box of salvation was a half-working terminal, an old-fashion touch screen job, the casing scratched and dull from who-knew-what.

"Sophia, you made us an opportunity and now I'm going to use it. Don't move, speak to no-one. I'll be as quick as possible."

"Chou, what are you doing? Don't leave me!"

But Chou was on the move, grabbing an abandoned, dented mug from under the camp bed, making her way like a wraith down the hall, away from the main hubbub of patients and staff. She was curious to see so many people injured in so short a space of time between docking on the station and now. Had the people resisted? Fought back? She paused at a sink and tried the tap, filled the cup with cold water that looked clear, but she was risking it being suitable for drinking. She approached a group of four women huddling together on the floor, pressing against the wall as if it could swallow them, take them any place else. Their eyes were hard, mouths set into thin lines. They met Chou's eye as she approached and accepted her mug offering in silence, nodded when they had all taken a sip. Chou continued down the line, offering it to each group, each person. Some ducked down and ignored her, others, like the women, stared her in the eye. All the time, Chou was counting down her internal clock, trying to stay calm despite feeling eyes on the back of her neck.

As she reached the last group of people, twins and a guardian, she offered them the cup and paused, tracking her progress with a slow eye. Nobody was watching her, the staff were dead on their feet and Chou only had to tap her arm against the scratched, dented ident reader and half her battle was done.

The terminal blinked into a monotone semblance of life, had a touchscreen that needed some heavy tapping before it would panic-inducingly load the next screen. *Intake: Personnel* and the screen went near-black with lists of names, real breathing people captured in this sector, and their fates. Chou double tapped, feeling like she would break the screen, one set of names that were all marked as 'Disposed'.

Now Chou looked at a list of the dead, a list of innocents all disposed of as if they were chaff. 'Deprived of vacuum' the notes read, and coordinates showing their last resting places. She took the pictma from her sleeve, took rolling film of the lists, coordinates, dates and took a deep breath, tried to relax the tension in her shoulders. It was nearly done, nearly time to report in. Hopefully they would be pleased with an early check-in.

With a reverence she didn't know she possessed, Chou replaced the pictma in her sleeve, straightened her jumper and turned around. A fight had broken out at the far end of the medical bay between two prisoners, both on the floor pummeling one another, rolling around in the drain, soaked through with the greasy waters of humanity. Chou walked back to Sophia's bed, hunkered down on the floor again. The Englishwoman seemed to be dozing, her fingers twitching in her sleep. Chou watched the fight evolve, one nurse talking into the comchip in his wrist. The far double doors of the bay opened and four guards burst onto the scene but these ones didn't have batons raised ready but instead were spitting tiny points of electricity from tasers. As they tackled the fighters, Chou began the process of checking in. She scratched the back of her neck and the tiny constellations scars there and felt the little pinprick of pain that was the comchip activating and sending a low frequency blip into the air waves. In theory these were so tiny that anybody monitoring those waves would miss it. Chou would not get a reply through the same channels: she would just have to wait and see if they would send her an extraction ship.

She watched the tail end of the fight, the adrenaline of her actions beginning to ebb and a bone-tiredness settling heavy across the whole of her body. With as soft a touch as possible, she replaced Sophia's out flung arm down the length of her body.

"You did good, English. I don't know what happens next."

"We'll have to stick together, then. Did you find Masami?" Sophia crossed her hands across her chest, turned her head to look at Chou with a weak smile.

"Er, yes. I've got a lead, but we'll have to be patient now, try and stay out of trouble. How's your head?"

"This must be how an egg feels when you crack it. Any chance of getting some water?"

"I'll get some, one moment." Chou helped Sophia raise herself onto her elbows, and the Englishwoman had three cups before the pain was too much. She lowered herself down with a groan, tried to get comfortable.

"Thank you, Chou. I wouldn't have survived in here."

"It was nothing. Now, try and sleep." Chou took Sophia's hand and gave it a squeeze, more for herself than she'd admit. The pair dozed as the medical bay emptied, a slow-draining swill of the desperate, lost and innocent.

Sophia exploded awake at the klaxon cry. The lights died as one and the gravity loosened its grip. There was screaming, shouting, confusion. A gentle suffusion of light cascaded down the walls, a backup generator kicking in somewhere. Sophia held onto her camp bed as it floated off the floor, looked around at Chou who was grimacing at the continuing klaxon. She was holding onto the cracked water mug, trying to stop the shaking in her hands.

There was a hiss and squeal as a voice came over a speaker system.

"This is Commander Fitzwilliam of Her Majesty's Space Militia. We have the station surrounded and are taking control of the systems. Gravity will be restored in three, two, one." Sophia crashed back to the floor, the shock flaring pain through her torso. She let out a cry, tears threatening to overspill. Chou sprawled onto the floor, letting go of the mug which tumbled into the drain.

"Oh god, it's the English! Chou, we're getting out!" Sophia was really crying now, out of relief, shock, pain.

"Just hold on, English."

From behind the far double doors came more shouting, somebody screaming in pain and a single, reckless gun shot. The medical staff were whispering to one another as they moved into the middle of the hall, hands raised. The doors burst open and camouflaged militia poured into the space, rifles raised. There was a beat of quiet before the main representative of the medical staff spoke.

"Please, we're just medical professionals captured from a previous raid. The command have our idents. Please, we're just trying to help people." He had a Welsh accent, was shaking with cold, panic or perhaps both. A shorter, thin white man wearing a dress uniform stepped out from behind the militia, removing his hat and holding it under his arm. He clicked his heels together and smiled around the bay.

"We will, of course, have to verify your story, but I'm sure we can have you on your way home sooner rather than later. My name is Private Blessedwater and I thank you for your patience with our investigations. Now, if I might ask you all to just hold tight a little longer while we finish clearing the rest of the station, that would be grand." To punctuate his point, there was a number of gunshots from back the way they'd appeared. En masse the soldiers turned as one, forming into two ranks all focused on the door. Private Blessedwater took no notice and instead stepped with a click of mirror-shined shoes over to Chou.

"Well, now, shall we begin with you, m'dear? Right this way. Your friend will be alright for five minutes by herself." He had one of those disarming smiles that was like an angler fish's light and Chou followed him out of the double doors and into a corner out of earshot.

"You called; we have answered. Give me the intel." And like that his smile dropped and Chou was looking down the gullet of the angler fish.

"I want to see Masami," she said, not quite looking him in the eye.

"And you will see her, mon petit, but first we need the intel. What did you find?"

"Lists of people brought through this sector, lists of people being… vented."

"My, my, that will be awkward to explain to the UN Council. Well done, little Raven, they will be pleased at the Tower. They may even have another job for you." Chou paused in handing over the pictma.

"I am not becoming one of your Ravens or working for the Tower. I was told to do one job and I've done it. Please, just let Masami go. She has nothing to do with your stupid war."

"You're wrong. She does have something to do with *this* war, and it's keeping you, a native

French speaker, in line. You will be indispensable, and if you want to see Masami again, I suggest you do exactly as you're told." Blessedwater took the pictma from Chou and tucked it into a pocket, a greasy smile seeping across his features.

"Now, mademoiselle, if you'll step this way for debriefing? And a change of clothes, maybe."

Chou looked at the double doors, let out a sigh and followed Blessedwater back into the medical bay. The smell of humanity was sour, and the lights were soft like the diffused light on a thinly clouded day.

The Duck Pond Incident

They say that it's runners who find the bodies. Or the walkers, panting and out of breath. The dog walkers too, watching with mixed parts fascination and horror as their beloved furry friend trots back ecstatic with their gory trophy.

But Jane had gotten around this by taking Terry - her black German Shepherd - around the duck pond and on through the park every day. There he could go for a little swim, pretend to be a duck and annoy the parents of the small children slowly killing the ducks with bread. Jane always took pleasure in the scowls of those parents when their small brats began to cry. Doubly so when Terry would then proceed to scrabble out of the water and shake, making the child scream even more. Terry was a good dog, though: loyal and obedient to a fault.

It was a crisp autumn day with a ground frost and sharp wind. Jane was pulling on her boots, wrapping her scarf about her face and patting her pockets for her front door keys when Terry bounded into the hall with his lead in his mouth.

"Walkies?" Jane trilled, hands on knees. Terry bumped his nose against her thigh with a whine, offering her the lead. She clipped it on and they set off at a slow pace towards the park.

Terry had come into Jane's life via her ex, Sadie, who had trained him from a puppy as a potential cadaver finding dog, and who had to make the decision that Terry wasn't cut out to be part of the service. They had met at one of the public meet-and-greets, where the ordinary public could see and speak to officers of the law and their teeth-filled partners. Followed by an awkward first date the next evening, as they'd just placed their drink orders when Sadie had gotten the call from work.

"I'm so sorry. Look, I'll phone you tomorrow? On-call has gone AWOL and they knew I had plans. Maybe I can wiggle something out of it." That something had been tickets to the aquarium where they'd held hands in the shark tunnel and looked up in wonder.

"Mummy, those ladies are holding hands!" The child's voice had echoed through the tunnel. Sadie smirked and they had moved on, spluttering and choking at the mother's face as it dawned on her that this would be the topic of conversation with her five-year old for the rest of the day.

But it wasn't to be. Jane and Sadie just hadn't clicked completely was all it was, and their lives were moving in very different directions. Terry had stayed, though, and was a welcome reminder of those few bliss-filled months.

They were coming up to the path that bisected a copse of birch and alder, the path a slippy crush of mouldering leaves. The river on their right, swollen and fast. The duck pond was very still though, a lazy splat-shaped body of murky water that was eroding its banks and spilling across the footpath. It was quiet today, with only a father and small child on the bank throwing fistfuls of crumbs to the overly enthusiastic collective of ducks, gulls, pigeons and a single moorhen.

Jane took Terry off his lead and he went to have a sniff and little wee amongst the trees. There were no squirrels to torment which disappointed him but he did double check the scent marks just to be sure. Satisfied with his brief wander amongst the copse, Terry began his investigation around the pond bank. He sniffed around the edge, leaving neat prints in the frosty mud and paused. He looked up, and cocked his head at Jane. They stared at each other for a moment, dog and human acknowledging the other's existence, before Terry snorted and belly flopped into the water.

He padded towards the ducks and gulls who had been enjoying their stodgy breakfast, and who then decided that a looming German Shepherd just ruined one's digestion. There followed a mass migration of ducks from water onto land, crowding around the child and its father to the screaming brat's delight.

Terry paddled towards the bank, almost mimicking a giant river otter. He stopped just short of the gathering of ducks and began to have a grand old sniff against the waterline. He started to paw at the bank, shattering the tranquility of the water's surface with looping waves of water cloudy with mud, lanky weeds and one abandoned plastic bottle.

"Terry! Come here!" But he doubled his efforts, ears flat against his head. The father was frowning at the large German Shepherd who was burrowing through filth and now starting to disturb the ducks. He did the shifty side-eye at Jane but deemed the situation not yet at the point where it was appropriate to interject and ask her to put her dog on the lead. He did pull back his child, though, by its little reins where it proceeded to fall on its bum in the mud and began to scream.

"Terry!" Jane took his lead from around her neck and stopped.

Terry was the colour of an oil slick, his coat saturated with water from the chest down. His ears twitched at Jane's call, but he ignored her and stuck his muzzle into the ragged hole he'd excavated. Then he began to tug and thrashed his head from side to side, churning up the water even more. The ducks and pigeons took off in a cloud of breadcrumbs and noise, flapping and squawking. And through the feathers, Jane saw what Terry had been digging out of the bank. She closed her eyes and pinched the bridge of her nose. She groaned from the pit of her stomach and began marching towards the scene. The father was staring with a wide, slack mouth and began to dry heave.

"Terry! Drop it!" Jane broke into a run. Terry thrashed the water with his tail and pricked his ears up, cocking his head to one side. His jaws dripped with pond water and slime from his prize. The father began to vomit and there was a little splash back onto Jane's boots.

"Terry, drop it. Drop it!" Jane knelt down in the mud and swallowed down nausea, trying to not smell Terry's treasure. She held out her hand and closed her eyes as Terry dropped the swollen, water-logged head into her hand.

"Good boy, Terry. Who's a good boy?" Jane took a great long mouth-breath, made the mistake of looking down at the head cupped in her hands, felt her fingers sinking through pond weed and mud.

"I'll phone the police." The father wiped his mouth on the back of his sleeve, spat onto the mud. He dragged his small child away from the pond, over the tiny little bridge that capped the weir and pulled out his phone. Jane frowned down at the head - a male she thought but couldn't be sure - and felt a calm sink into her bones. Not a tiredness from emotional upheaval, but a calm and contentedness that felt a little out of place considering the circumstances. Terry was still looking up at her, his big brown eyes full of pride as he thrashed his tail from side to side.

Several police vehicles arrived thirty minutes later, bringing with them bright tape to cordon off the scene, officers wading into the pond to probe the bank for the rest of the body. Jane handed the head off to a formless person in a white forensics overall who spirited it away to keep the evidence from spoiling more than it had. She kept Terry on a very short leash, made him sit down right next to her, and the pair waited for the first officer who had been on scene to come back to take a statement.

"Well this is a turn up for the books." Sadie sidled up to Jane, her hands bundled in the heavy leash of a tan and black German Shepherd who plonked himself down next to Terry.

"Hi. Um, how are you doing?"

"I'm okay. You?" Sadie gave her dog a scratch behind the ears, sneaking him a treat from her pocket.

"Yeah, I'm okay. Good thing I didn't have any plans today. Who's this?"

"Rigby. He's nearly finished his training and I'll be handing him off in a couple of weeks if he passes, but I thought today would be good practice for him." The two women gave a smile and Sadie chuckled as Terry recognised her and gave a small whine. She got on her knees and fondled Terry's ears. He attempted to lick her face, but she pushed him down.

"Listen," she said, taking a mighty interest in the pad of Terry's paw, "I was thinking, they're having a *Police Academy* double-bill at that tiny cinema on Cheap Street. It's on Friday night and I've got a spare ticket, if you were interested? I mean, only if you wanted to go that is. I just thought that maybe-" here she trailed off, blushed and started to rub Terry's chest.

"Sure, I would like that." Jane grinned and felt

butterflies stir in her chest. Maybe it wasn't sure a bad thing that Terry had found a body after all.

Stand Tall

The rain's whispering was dying down to a sigh on the wind and Lacerta stood at the entrance to her cave with her legs spread, her arms crossed, tasting the air with her forked-tongue. She was a round, black woman with a penchant for sensible clothes: blouses and bras and hoes, but allowed herself a little colour in the head scarfs she used to tame her beautiful, curly hair when she was working. A clattering on the wind drifted up from the valley's floor and she tiptoed to the edge of the plateau outside her cave, peered down from on high and frowned at what she saw, the delicate, blue-black scales around her eyes sliding together. A long train of wagons that were in the last stages of curling into a tight circle just outside the village, with pages and grooms and other people scattering with poles and long lengths of canvas. Visitors? Here? The markets were not due for months yet. It wasn't even time for the main harvest.

Lacerta tucked herself back into her cave where it was cozy with the smell of woodsmoke and drying herbs. She began to gather and pack her dirty laundry, deciding to make time for herself and her needs for once. The secret creek a little further up the mountain would be bloated, ripe for washing clothes.

She tasted the air again, found a new scent there, the scent of sweat and horses and there followed a shout, her name on the wind. Lacerta decided to ignore them: she had not moved into her dry cozy cave to serve the village people but to live a life of her choosing, independent and free. However, she had to admit in her heart, that these people had helped by bringing her small food parcels; herbs; wool and linen when it was going spare. And they hadn't cast her out for her knowledge, for helping deliver their babies and treating their sick.

"Lacerta! I know you're home." The shouting was coming closer, coming up the track that wound its way up through the woods that lay around the mountain's flanks, continued, twisting and meandering up the side of the mountain to her cave. Lacerta rolled her eyes, admonished herself for not getting up to the creek quick enough, and peered out the cave.

"Sasha, you'll wake the dead with your incessant howling. What's the matter?" Sasha was nearly twice Lacerta's height, nearly twice as wide too, tanned from his long days in the fields. He was frowning at the gangly boy he'd guided up the track, who was panting and blowing with the exertion. He was dressed in black, his surcoat stitched with the king's crest picked out in gold. Lacerta's eyes lingered on the crest - an eagle gripping a snake in its talons - and a little drop of ice worked its way into her heart.

"Lacerta," Sasha dipped his head, "I told them that you don't just do house calls and there's a standard-"

"It's fine, Sasha, thank you for bringing our guest here. Please return to your business."

"You'll be okay?" He rubbed his thumb across the scar that zigzagged from the corner of his mouth.

"Yes, thank you." Lacerta waited until Sasha was out of sight down the path and into the fringe of the wood before turning her full attention on the stranger.

"What can I do for the king?" she asked, "as Sasha has informed you, I am not here at anybody's beck and call, royalty or otherwise."

"His majesty bid you attend him. He's sick with something his own physician can't cure and would have outside help." The messenger handed over a tattered piece of parchment.

"How shall I refer to you?" She unfurled the parchment, pretending she didn't see the look of hope on the youth's face.

"My name's Ali. I'm a boy, you see."

"Very well, Ali, so it shall be." The king's handwriting was little more than a scrawl, almost as if he was ill-practised with his letters. He bid she attend him at once and it was finished with a fancy wax seal that must have meant something in other circles. Lacerta raised an eyebrow ridge.

"Very well then. Let me fetch my healer's tricks and we can call upon his majesty."

Ali was very open and chatty once he'd gotten beyond Lacerta's forward manner and odd appearance. The page skipped down the track, nimble as a goat, always a few steps ahead of the wisewoman. Lacerta let the boy rattle on, remembering a time when she had been as light-hearted. Ali showed more caution as they reached the edge of the wood. It was not unpleasant in the sun-dappled wood, with patches of bluebells and an overlaying chorus of bird song. Only the shadowed nooks amongst the trunks lurked with a sinister purpose.

"Come on, she's just being melodramatic. Didn't you leave an offering on the way up?" Lacerta ploughed on, taking the lead.

"No? Was I supposed to?" Ali took hold of the woman's elbow, helping her over patches of ferns.

"Let go of me, silly boy. No, you don't have to leave an offering to the lady but she prefers it. Do you not do this in your village?"

"I'm a city boy, ma'am." Lacerta nodded as if the mystery of the universe had been revealed to her. They marched on through the woods in a respectful quiet, although Ali was bursting with questions. He nearly stepped into an ant's nest and Lacerta stopped.

"Ask it," she snapped, but not unkindly.

"What happened to your tongue?" Lacerta frowned, drawing her eyebrow ridges down towards the bridge of her nose. She slowly poked her tongue out, extending it to its full length, until it hung nearly down to her hips. She flicked it in the air, tasting a little of Ali's fear and excitement. Then she rolled it up with a flick and grinned.

"I was born with it."

"Nobody is born with a lizard's tongue, ma'am." Lacerta laughed and continued the march on through wildflower beds.

"If you say so."

The King's Progress was always an event of pomp and circumstance. For all the grumblings about taxes and long winters, being stuck on the outskirts of the kingdom and prone to raiding parties from their less than hospitable neighbours, the villagers in the mountains did enjoy having a good look at all of the finery attached to such a retinue.

Twenty-five wagons were pulled up in a circle on the valley floor, horses checked for thrown shoes, small children running around screaming and daring each other to approach the fringe of the woods. Ali led Lacerta amongst a small throng of dusty children who whispered behind their hands. She raised an eyebrow ridge at them, curling the corners of her mouth into a smile as they screamed and ran away, laughing.

The pair made their way to the largest wagon, painted black and embellished with the king's crest. It was drawn by a team of four, stamping and snorting in gleaming harness. Ali stopped short of the door, straightened his surcoat and smoothed his hair back under his little cap. Taking a deep breath, he reached out and rapped on the door twice. It exploded outwards as an older man in black robes breezed out. He was muttering under his breath, but stopped short as he caught sight of Lacerta. He barked and shook his head.

"Now they've summoned a wisewoman? What good will that do?"

"Stop your whining, doctor." Ali waved him off.

"Mark my words, girl, I have done everything possible."

"Not a girl." Ali turned his back on the doctor and walked up the three short steps into the wagon. Lacerta watched the doctor walk away. Her face screwed up as if she'd sucked on something bitter.

"That was just plain rude," she muttered and followed Ali up the steps. "Do you get that a lot?" she whispered.

"He does it deliberately. Thinks that people can't change, you know? His majesty tries, with my pronouns and name I mean, and that gives me hope." Ali cleared his throat and took a small breath. "Your majesty, announcing Lacerta, wisewoman and healer from the local village." Ali bowed deeply at the waist.

The interior of the wagon had been split out into quarters using tapestries and throws. The skylight in the roof had been thrown open to let in the air. The king was tucked up in a large bed, a cold compress across his brow, his breathing slow and ragged. For a king, he looked small and frail, not the regal, proud image stamped on the odd coin that came Lacerta's way. His black skin was covered in a thin film of sweat and his baby dreads had been tied back out of his face. He opened his eyes, looked confused for a moment like he wasn't where he expected to be.

"Ali?" he sighed, a cough hacking its way up from his lungs as the compress fell from his brow. The page knelt down by the bed, held the compress until the king's coughing had lessened and replaced it.

"Yes, my king. I'm sorry that we woke you." Ali looked up at Lacerta, still hovering in the doorway, beseeching her to help. The wisewoman puffed up her chest with a big breath, got on her knees next to Ali and took the king's hand. She wasn't usually one for using titles and pleasantries, but this was a delicate matter and she decided to tread carefully.

"Your majesty-"

"Darius," he whispered.

"Your majesty, I need to ask you some questions about your illness and then, with your permission, I would like to examine you."

"My physician-"

"Is rude and lazy. I can't help you with second-hand information, majesty." Ali's eyes widened at Lacerta's bluntness, but Darius began to chuckle.

"Very well, examine me, ask me your questions."

Lacerta's examination took as long as it needed to take, listening to the king's breathing, measuring his pulse, examining his eyes and tongue. She only asked him the occasional question, to save his coughing and to reduce the discomfort.

"It's not life threatening," she concluded, helping Darius to lie back down. "I have a remedy to ease your discomfort and to help you sleep, but your body needs to fight this which means lots of rest, lots of sleep."

It also meant that the Progress would be hanging around for maybe a week, eating up the village's food and their other resources. The locals weren't going to appreciate their hard work and graft going to line somebody else's stomach, especially with the light dying a little more each day as the summer crept on.

But that was a conversation for later and she set about rummaging through her healer's kit for ingredients, filling the wagon with the smell of herbs with just an edge of garlic and precious lemon peel, bright and refreshing. She mixed it up with watered down wine and helped the king to sit up again to drink.

"Please stay. Ali can find you a place to sleep," he whispered as his eyes fluttered close. Lacerta shared a look with Ali, quiet all through the examination, waiting for the king's breathing to deepen. Lacerta packed up her kit, placed a finger on her lips, and cracked the wagon door open an inch to look out before slipping out with the page behind her. They closed the door with the softest click and descended the three little steps to the grass.

"Will he be okay?" Ali whispered.

"If he can get the rest he needs, yes. It's just bad flu at the moment, but if he doesn't let his body heal itself, it'll get worse." Ali nodded and bit his lip, worried. There was a rumble like thunder from across the ring of wagons, a rolling, whispering thunder that died out with the sound of cheers and clapping.

"Ser Jasper and the other knights. He holds the command while his majesty recovers," Ali explained.

"And he spends his time doing what exactly?" Lacerta listened to another roll of thunder, a great splintering of horse-backed lances and could taste sweat on the air.

"Ser Jasper is the king's champion."

"And yet he does not come to defend our mountain passes when our neighbours come raiding in the spring." Lacerta shook her head, rubbed the fine scales around her eyes - a tic she had not quite shaken - and hoisted up her healer's bag. "I'm sorry, that was uncalled for. Show me where I will be sleeping."

Lacerta spent three days in the Progress camp. Its presence nearly destroyed the tiny village's livelihood. The wood was nearly depleted of the deer and boar; the wild mountain goats milked dry; farm spouses bothered for eggs and chickens and fleece. The king's knights would get rowdy in the public house. Whispers abounded amongst the village folk that anybody found on the road home after dark would come to mischief, so people kept to themselves behind locked doors.

And the noise and smell of the camp caused Lacerta great discomfort. She was a woman of peace and reflection, enjoyed her own company over the petty intrigues and games that came with the royal court. She shuddered to think what life in the capital was like. She yearned to return to her cave and finally get her laundry done. It was before dawn on the fourth day in camp. Even the birds were still asleep, the only awake souls, Lacerta and the guards, huddled in their cloaks against the chill. Lacerta passed between tents and covered-wagons in silence, her feet silent against what little grass remained of the field. She was thirsty, but needed to make water badly as well. Coming up to the latrine trench, she paused. There was a large bundle in the mud, a bundle that rocked a little and snuffled. Lacerta's boot scuffed against the earth and the bundle froze, silent, before making an effort to sit up.

"Ali!" Lacerta's heart lurched in her chest at the sight of the child, face streaked with dirt and blood, his eye swollen shut and lip split. Ali's face crumbled into tears and Lacerta wrapped her arms around him, pulled him to her in a tight embrace.

"Who did this?" Lacerta growled. She held him at arm's length to take stock of his injuries, bit her tongue against the rage rising in her belly, chest, throat at the sight of the child, beaten, stripped and forced into a dress.

"They said that I needed to start acting like a girl my age, that this phase had gone on long enough. They took my clothes, beat me." Ali's croak opened up into sobs again. He put his face in his hands, flinched at the rawness of his wounds.

"Ali, tell me who did this. We must report this otherwise they'll win. How dare they tell you you're a girl? That isn't their decision to make." She took her crumpled handkerchief from her sleeve, patted away Ali's tears with a feather's touch, let the boy blow his nose. He took a deep shuddering breath, bigger than Lacerta believed his lungs could hold. And then, heavy like a death peal of a bell, Ali whispered, "his majesty's knights. Four of them; Ser Jasper and his friends." Lacerta's eye ridges came together in a frown and she flicked her tongue out twice, three times. She could taste the stench of the latrine trench, Ali's blood, sweat and tears, taste her own sweat from a lack of bathing.

"Okay, Ali, okay. We'll get this sorted. But first, I need a piss."

The walk through the camp towards the wood and mountain was quiet. Nobody hailed them as they slipped beyond the camp boundary and melted into the wood, Lacerta letting her feet take the lead. The knot in Lacerta's chest loosened and she was surprised by the relief, hadn't really realised she'd been holding onto so much tension. She guided Ali towards the deer track that was steep, but secret. By the time they had reached the plateau outside Lacerta's cave, they were blowing hard and had to stand for a few minutes to catch their breath, heads thrown back as they watched the stars slip away into the coming dawn.

Her cave was a welcome sight. The fire had died with nobody to tend it, but her herbs and food stores were where they'd been left; her cave was still her safe space. She found clean, comfortable clothes for Ali.

"I've no shoes'll fit you, but it's not too rocky here abouts with the grass. Let's get you cleaned up."

Lacerta guided Ali around the shoulder of the mountain as the first rose-peach rays of the dawn peeked over the horizon. The shoulder of the mountain hid a narrow, steep gully that was carpeted in soft grasses, wild flowers and wild oats. Twisting around a corner, they came upon the wide creek shaded by weeping willows and birches, a peaceful place that only the animals and Lacerta knew about. Ali stripped out of the dress and ran into the centre of the water, finding a pool to crouch in, covering his bruised body up to his neck in the chilly water. Lacerta let the boy have some space, stacked their clean clothes and towels on a natural shelf made by tree roots.

Keeping one eye on Ali in his pool, Lacerta stretched her arms up, shut her eyes and just breathed in fresh, clean air, filling her lungs up as much as possible before letting it all go. And then she began to think.

Lacerta considered the effects of the Progress's upheaval on the village, and worried over the coming winter months: would they recover enough food and hides for the snows, or would this be a year where people starved to death? An anger bloomed in her chest. It was nobody's fault that the king was so sick, but his Progression couldn't just stop where it pleased. Notice had to be given, preparations made, there must have been somewhere else for them to stop. Not her village. She smiled at that. For all her wanting to keep them at arm's length, she had let them in after all.

She decided that after the Progress's departure she would speak to the village leaders to see about taking a stock of the materials left, to start thinking about the winter months now, even before the main harvest had been brought in. But right now, in this instance, she turned her attentions back to Ali, still submerged in the chill of the pool.

"Has this happened before?" she asked, breaking the cool of the water and the birdsong. Ali shook his head.

"People have been nasty before, but through words or by refusing me food. It's the first time anybody's hit me. I thought people would have left me alone if I dressed and acted like a boy, that they wouldn't care what was in my breeches." Ali looked down at his body and frowned.

"People have their own minds made up about how things should be and sometimes if something doesn't fit their way of thinking, they panic. And this happens." Lacerta waved her hand at Ali, taking in his injuries. "And that's wrong. People are lazy and won't try and learn, listen to you. They want everything laid out in front of them."

"I won't let it stop me being me, though. My name is Ali and I am a boy!" He thrust his fists into the air, shut his eyes and tilted his head back into the sun's first strong rays of the day.

Lacerta had a quick scrub herself in the creek, watching the water's surface turn grey and oily from three days of wood smoke, sweat and dirt. She rinsed off a little further upstream, felt how clean and refreshed she was not only in her body, but also her soul. She stood up and ran her hands over her body to brush off the excess water, smoothed down her eyebrow ridges, looked down at her thighs, at the crooked lines of scars faint against her midnight-dark skin. She shut those memories down, refused to let them ruin the peace of mind and body in this exact moment. She slipped up the bank and took clean clothes from Ali who had shut his eyes and gone bright red.

"Your back is stripy like a tiger. Were your born with that too. I mean beside your tongue?" He peeked to see if Lacerta was dressed.

"No, those scars were given to me a while ago now. People fear what they don't understand or think they can control it." She slipped into her clothes, twisted her hair into a small knot and tucked it under her headscarf, clean and plain. For a moment she shut her eyes and breathed in deep, breathed in until she felt her chest would burst and then let it all out in one long burst.

"Let's get your wounds clean, and I want to check your teeth too. Then we'll see about going back. I need to check on Darius." Ali nodded and, nimble as a mountain goat, skipped and ran back down the hidden track to Lacerta's cave. Lacerta followed at a slower pace, mulling over their next steps.

It was clear that the Progress would have to move on, otherwise the village was not going to recover their losses before the growing season was over. She made a mental note to check her herb harvest sites in the wood, to make sure she'd have cures enough for coughs and colds. But what about the boy? She could not patch him up and send him back to people who wished him harm. Her heart squeezed in her chest: they might kill him. She shook her head to banish these thoughts. At the end of the gully, the mountain's shoulder dropped away and she could see out over the valley, the edge of the wood and on the plain, the camp. It was busy with people and fires and livestock being led to pasture. And the tiny village clustered amongst all this, up to the edge of the wood, down to the plain, almost split in half by this new camp, a wedge between their way of life and the outside world, a world of intrigue and games.

Ali was already pottering about the cave, setting a new fire and fetching a pot for water.

"There's water in that butt in the corner. Ali, what do you want to do in life? If you could do anything?" She began to pick dry herbs from their bundles, putting some in the pot for boiling, looking for her mortar and pestle to pulp the others for Ali's wounds.

"I want to be a knight." Lacerta paused and looked at Ali with a frown.

"Really?"

"Yes! Ser Jasper and his friends aren't real knights, even with their spurs and horses and their finery. They have no honour. Knights are supposed to help and protect people, not sneak about and beat up little boys." He hooked the pot over the fire and stood with his back to Lacerta. She let him have a little snuffle and cry - not from sadness or fear, but from frustration - while she pounded herbs and a little precious oil. The cave was cozy with the fire casting a strong light over the shelves holding Lacerta's healing materials.

"I mean, I know I'm too old to start now in a traditional sense. You have to be eight to be a page? And then squire at fourteen? But if I can find a hedge knight to apprentice with, I thought I still have a chance. And with a hedge knight at least I'd get to go travelling, meet all kinds of people, get out of the court." He paused to prod the fire a little, watched the water begin to simmer. "Don't get me wrong," he whispered to the fire nook, "the court has fed and clothed me, but it's not where I belong, where I can be me."

"I think a lot of people would agree with you there." Lacerta sprinkled a pinch of salt into the mush of herbs and oil, mixed it in with her little finger before tasting the air with her tongue. Perhaps a touch too much oil but it would do the job. She looked at Ali and sighed.

"Let's get your wounds tended, otherwise your face will drop off. Come and sit here where I can get at you. This will sting but it just means that the healing is started, okay?" She dabbed spots of the mulch around Ali's eye to mark out the boundary before spreading them in a wide curve. Being as gentle as possible she covered the whole left half of Ali's face in the bitter smelling concoction. Ali bit down on his lip against the nettle-like sting and took deep breaths.

"This hurts more than their beating," he whispered, but he smiled a little.

"Open your mouth, I want to check your teeth, make sure they're not loose. Stick your tongue out. No, your teeth look fine."

There was a scrabbling from outside, shouting. A village boy poked his head into the cave.

"Quick! They've taken Sasha! Come quickly!"

"Who's taken Sasha?"

"The king's men!"

"I'll be along." The boy fled and Lacerta took a precious moment to meet Ali's eye.

"You can stay here," she said.

"No, I'm coming with you." He unhooked the water pot from its hook and left it on a brick. Lacerta scraped the last of the mush from the mortar and capped it in a clay jar. She tucked it into her healer's bag and topped it up with more herbs for cuts, bruises and to stem blood flow.

"Will Sasha be okay?"

"He's a hot-headed impulsive fool, but he's tougher than most. Any idea where they will have taken him?"

"There's a little cell kept near the latrine."

"Quick, then, Ser Knight, lead on."

Sasha had not gone quietly. He had broken one guardsman's nose with his fist, another guardswoman's with his head. He had taken a chair, one of the precious few in his possession, and had slammed it over another head, thrashed and bitten and punched as the king's guard had attempted to lay hands on him. It was only when the sword was placed against his throat that he had stopped, heaving for breath. They had forced his neck and wrists into irons and dragged him into the street like a mongrel. At first he had shouted and resisted, demanding to know his crime, but they beat him until he was silent. The village people watched from their doorways, from around corners. Pinched lips and frowns followed the guards through the village and the silence of the watchers was absolute. Soon the villagers were following Sasha and the guards, in little groups of twos and threes, peeling off the sides of the low buildings. The guards kept their eyes front and centre on their prisoner and tried to keep their breathing easy.

They reached the edge of the camp without incident, the guards bolder now they were back amongst their own people, but their bluster disappeared when they glanced back to see the villagers still following them, the group getting larger and larger. The camp people stopped their mending and cooking to watch the oncoming tide. Nobody spoke until the guards stopped by the jail cell lashed to the bed of a wagon. The captain took the manacles from Sasha and he was pushed into the cell, the door clanged shut and locked.

"What are you doing with Sasha?" This from a woman in the crowd, but the guards couldn't see who had spoken. The captain cleared his throat and found his voice from somewhere.

"This man was caught attempting to start a fire," he told the crowd. They glanced at one another, unimpressed.

"How else you supposed to boil water for breakfast?"

"No, I mean, start a fire here in camp. The blaze would have destroyed everything." Captain Jardin had held his position as captain of the guard for twenty-three years and had seen near-revolution but never had he been so unnerved by a crowd of people.

"But he didn't, so no harm done. Why don't you let Sasha go now, and we'll see to him, yeah?" The woman stepped to the front of the crowd, bald and dressed in a motley of colours. Jardin shook his head.

"This man is under arrest for attempted arson and attempting to harm the king and until he is cleared of these charges he will remain here. Now, I suggest you leave."

There was a rustle in the crowd, murmurs sweeping through it, making it sway and rock like a choppy sea. Jardin turned back to his squad, beckoned them closer and lowered his voice, "keep an eye on them. If they try anything." He drew his thumb across his neck and the guards nodded, took up positions either side of the cell. Those who'd been broken in the fracas slipped off to find a physician, grateful for an excuse to be anywhere but here. Jardin turned to face the crowd one more time before marching off to the jousting field to find the acting authority.

Lacerta found the crowd tucked into the camp, muttering amongst themselves. She tapped Peter Mal's shoulder.

"What's happened?"

"They've arrested Sasha for attempted arson. Says he won't be released until he's cleared. These soft people waltz in like they own the place, take our food and materials without any useful compensation and then beat Sasha and drag him out of his own home. Honestly, Lacerta, they need to leave. Is there anything you can do?"

"I'll see what can be done to release Sasha and get them moved on, Peter. Just keep an eye on this lot. The last thing we need is panic." She patted him on the shoulder and began to slip through the crowd, people parting for her and the boy. Ali looked into people's faces, watched their expressions as they noticed his face, his split lip and swelling eye. Lacerta made it to the front of the crowd and pulled Ali close.

"Are these the knights who attacked you?" she whispered.

"No, these are the king's guard, Katherine, the other Paul. They're okay, I guess."

"Stay here and watch the crowd, I'm going to try and see Sasha, make sure he's okay." She straightened her blouse and carried her hessian bag of herbs and heals in front of her as if it were a shield. She bobbed a small curtsey.

"Please, let me see him and tend his wounds."

"Nobody is to see the prisoner until after the hearing."

"Katherine, listen to me and look at this crowd. You have taken one of their own by force, locked him a cell and now you won't let a healer see to him? Please, be reasonable."

"We are being reasonable, witch. Now get back or I will have you removed."

"I beg your pardon?"

"You heard me." Katherine lowered her halberd and stepped forward one pace. Paul swallowed and followed suit. For a moment, the crowd held its breath and then it exploded into noise and movement. It surged forward, shouting, making demands, pressing up against Lacerta's back, pushing her forward. She spread her arms wide and pushed back, shouted at them to stop, but they weren't listening. All of their frustrations and fears collected over the last days were spilling over. Ali was by her side and she drew him close, wrapped an arm about him. He turned to Paul and shouted, "Paul, please. Let us see to Sasha and they'll calm down"

"What happened to your face?"

"Ser Jasper happened. Paul, listen to me. Let us see to Sasha." The guard shook his head, licked his lips, stamped his feet back and forth like a skittish horse.

"What are we going to do?" Ali looked up at Lacerta and she gave him a small smile.

"We will be patient and wait," she said and looked at Katherine, letting the growing anger of the crowd infect her a little, the noise filling her ears and mind.

It wasn't long before Captain Jardin came back with a tall, broad white man who was wearing full plate armour. He wore a longsword at his hip. Moving between Katherine and Paul he raised his hands, appealing for calm.

"Peace! Let us have peace! I am Ser Jasper, king's champion and protector of the innocent. What is the meaning of this?"

"You have arrested this man on flimsy pretences and won't let me see to his injuries." Lacerta approached Ser Jasper with her hands held up in a gesture of peace, the swell of the crowd at her back. She was nearly standing on the knight's sabatons.

"The captain tells me he has made himself quite clear on the matter. You can see this man when he has been cleared by the king for attempted arson."

"And how long will that take? The king is sick and needs his rest, needs sleep. You cannot expect Sasha to stay locked up like this." A roll of agreement from the crowd and the slightest rise of an eyebrow from the knight. His hand rested on the pommel of his sword.

"I suggest you watch your tone, herbwoman. This man is subject to the laws of the land, the laws of the king," he muttered to her.

"Don't you dare speak to her like that!" Sasha's voice rang out strong and clear, despite his bloodied face and hands. "You blow through this valley, unannounced, uninvited and you take our food without giving anything in return except for useless coin. What use have we for coin so far from your precious capital? Coin won't fill hungry bellies or keep us warm in the depths of winter. I was starting that fire so you'd leave!"

There was a lull in the noise as the people listened to Sasha, nodding in agreement because all of their hard work since the ground had thawed had been for nothing. The first stone was cast and struck Ser Jasper on the chest; it did nothing, didn't hurt, but the floodgates holding back the crowd opened and they overran the guards, throwing stones and anything else that came to hand. Lacerta pulled Ali from the crush, barged her way through the mass towards a gap between tents, out into the open, hoping to get away but the crowd was dispersing through the camp, pulling down tents, kicking over fires, all to a background of screaming and shouting. Somewhere a bell began to ring and there was thunder in the air. Lacerta heard the snorting of horses and fear dropped into her belly like ice. The knights were charging from their jousting practice to the aid of their champion who had been swept under when the crowd surged. She watched as, with lances lowered, the knights breezed through the people, striking them, trampling them, watched as they came towards her, the lance tip a clenched fist. Ali tugged on her sleeve, forced her to roll between tents.

"Ali, I have to help the people, my people. We need to stop this before any more life is wasted."

"No! They'll kill you."

Thunder passed down the avenue on the other side of the tent, rolled away and stopped. Over the noise of battle came a high whistle. Lacerta peered through the gap to see the knights rounded up, their horses panting and snorting. The king had a silver whistle in his mouth, and he was counting those gathered around him. Ser Jasper limped towards his people, holding his arm where it had been crushed beneath the villagers' stampede. Lacerta crossed the space between them and, not thinking, drew herself up to her full height and turned on Darius.

"Is this how you treat those you are sworn to protect? With violence and death?" she snapped.

"Watch your tongue, witch, or I'll cut it out of your mouth and feed it to my dogs." Ser Jasper drew his eating knife from his belt and brandished its point at her.

"No! I will not be silenced. You beat up small boys and run down helpless villagers and have the audacity to speak to me in such a way? How dare you? I demand that this whole Progress clears out."

"You demand? Hark at you, a herbwoman skulking in a stinking cave."

Lacerta heaved in a breath, resisting the urge to punch the knight full in the face.

"I am not just a herbwoman. I am the one who has put his majesty on his path to health. I am the one who saw to your wounded after brawling at our tavern. Do not try me, Ser Jasper." Her cheeks were flushed, but she met Ser Jasper's eye and held it.

"With your permission, I would like to remove the dead and injured to where I can treat them, including Sasha." She turned her gaze on Darius, pale with a sheen of sweat across his brow from where he was still sick. He sighed and Lacerta noticed for the first time the lines etched into his face from the weight of ruling so many people, of having to keep touch with so many elements like Ser Jasper. He nodded his head at her as Ser Jasper began to shout and rage against Lacerta's attitude. She walked away a few steps, head held high, before pausing and turning back towards Darius.

"Also, I think you need to look for a new page. Ali will be staying with me for a little while until I can get him settled."

Ashes to Ashes

It was eleven AM on Tuesday morning and all was peace in Ginger Tabby Books. A restful peace of quiet reflection as the rain pattered down the window and Amelina's one customer shifted his weight from one foot to the other; a small, soft gesture that may have not been entirely conscious.

Amelina was loathe to break the tranquil world of the shop, but it *was* Tuesday and the orders from the weekend were now stacked neatly under the counter ready for collection. She would wait for her customer to leave before picking up the phone.

It was quite unfortunate when her solo customer replaced one book - a book Amelina still thought about weeks after having finished it - and selected the chunky volume beside it. She paused, hands on the counter, counting backwards from five and, sure enough, her customer began to sneeze. Huge explosive sneezes that had a large white (stained) handkerchief to match. It was impressive watching him continue sneezing - nine times in a row, ten - while fumbling the book back into its place on the shelf. He waved a hand apologetically and burst out into the rain. His sneezes faded into the distance, leaving Amelina alone.

"Twelve is your new record," she said. Now that the peaceful air was shattered, she booted up the playlist compiled for quiet browsing, a compilation of classic composers that Amelina had only vaguely heard about from University Challenge.

"I don't know why you stock that rubbish. It'd rot his brain."

The music dipped and swirled as a cold breath cooled the back of Amelina's neck. She shuddered and took a moment to compose herself before turning around.

Mx. Smith was in their middle thirties, grey and drawn, wearing a frilly shirt and skinny jeans with steel-toed boots. The brightest spot was the white streak in their slicked-back fringe which, when Amelina had been brave enough to ask, apparently happened when they fell out of a tree.

"Listen, people read different things and if we want the shop to stay afloat, we need to stock the kind of thing they'll pay for."

"But-"

"No! This is, first and foremost, a business. It needs to pay the bills same as anybody else." Mx. Smith mumbled at that, settled onto the counter. The music dipped again, slowed and stopped.

"I didn't mean to snap. I, just, it's been stressful lately and it wasn't fair to take it out on you."

"S'alright. I forgive you. I'll try harder in future. Who knows what'll happen if this place closes?"

"Probably be turned into flats."

"Then I would have the pleasure of spoiling milk and seeing naked bodies in the shower." They both grimaced at the thought. Mx. Smith let out a sigh and drifted to the stacks, selecting a volume at random before disappearing through the ceiling to the reading nook. Amelina took a deep breath, leant the heels of her hands against the edge of the counter and stretched out her back.

"We'll get there," she whispered and picked up the phone to begin the round of customer calls.

Amelina had only been temping at the shop for exactly one week when Mx. Smith's ashes were delivered. It was the most peculiar parcel she had been handed and wasn't sure of the correct procedure to follow. The solicitor had removed a small sheaf of paper from her briefcase and reminded a flabbergasted Mr. Isaacs that he had indeed signed permission for her client's ashes to be scattered on the property.

"Well, er, of course. If that's the letter of the law. Might I suggest the rooftop garden?"

So, it was Amelina, Mr. Isaacs and the solicitor to witness Mx. Smith's send-off on a cloudy Wednesday morning. The wind picked up as the lid came off the urn and the ashes rose in a cloud. Amelina licked the ash from her lips, an unconscious action that she didn't register until later when looking at her reflection in the staff toilet mirror, washing the film of Mx. Smith from her face to swirl and gurgle down the plughole.

Amelina had never given any conscious thought to her own brief existence: was this it? Scrape together enough money for rent each month, only to end up partly washed down a plughole? She'd beaten that particular line of thinking off by drinking her flatmate's bargain vodka that night, until she passed out on the sofa, playing dead.

Wednesday was bleak, overcast with a growl of thunder in the air. Amelina would either have a full shop, or a dead shop. There would be no in-between. Whichever way it went, she would still need to prepare for the day ahead. She decided on the medium set of gold hoops, braided her hair but couldn't find the energy to apply any make-up. Picking up the limp salad out of the fridge on the way out, she wondered where she was supposed to find the energy to finish it later. It was when she was unlocking the shop door that the first drop of rain fell, straight onto her nose. The deluge opened as she was putting out the sign, the thunder snapping and the lightning freezing everything for a blink. Amelina settled in over a cup of peppermint tea, leaning against the counter and watching the waterfall stream down the window. Her carefully selected display would be reduced to blurs of bold colours, but it would still hopefully attract the occasional lonely, drowning soul.

"Amelina, do we have the next book in this series?" Mx. Smith popped their head through the floor, by Amelina's boots and held the book up over their head.

"Let me check. I take it you enjoy the way gender was presented throughout?"

"It was a refreshing look at it, yes. I admire her writing style a lot, actually. I had aspired to similar things myself." Mx. Smith took up their customary space on the counter, crossing their ankles and kicking forward and back. Amelina replaced the book - unmarked, still perfect and unread to any mortal eye - and bit her lip as she scanned the shelves.

"It might be downstairs. Watch the shop for me." Amelina stomped down to the stockroom, chilled and gloomy, woke up the internal computer to search for the next book. It was one she hadn't read just yet, so maybe after Mx. Smith had finished with it, Amelina might loan it to herself. They did have a copy, right in the back, where she still meant to replace the dead tubelight, another thing still on her to-do list.

A series of sneezes filtered down through the gloom, making her start a little: a customer, first thing on a thundery, biblical shower type of morning? She clattered back up the stairs, leaving the book on a corner table for Mx. Smith to find and exploded behind the counter with a smile.

"Good morning! Can I help you?" Her customer was actually two white men, damp, short dark hair curling from the moisture in the air. Their dull raincoats dripped onto her beautifully swept, pristine floor, but at least they weren't shaking out umbrellas all over the stock.

"Hi, yeah, I need a book for my niece who's turning eight. I wanted something fun, but educational. Maybe a history book?"

"Sure, let me show you my favourite kid's history book." Amelina guided her customer around the corner into the children's and teens' section, leaving the other guy to just browse in fiction, quietly dripping. Mx. Smith peered from below the counter, narrowing their eyes at this lonesome man. They had a funny feeling, weren't sure of them - especially as he was less interested in the books and more in the shop door and its lock. He took a little, jaunty stroll downstairs to non-fiction, peeped around the office door and a slow smile spread across his lips. He took out his phone and sidled into the office, taking quick snaps of the back door, the desk lock, the computer. Mx. Smith stirred the cockles of their heart into a smouldering burn and extended their very essence into the spinning motes in the air, extending and pushing them up the creep's nose. It wasn't long before he was sneezing and spluttering, coughing into his hands. He fled upstairs as Amelina was finishing her sale. The pair left, letting in a cool breeze as they opened the door and melted into the rain.

"Amelina, those men are no good. While you were up here, his mate was in the office, taking pictures, canvassing the place."

"You're sure? I can't go to the police and say, 'Hey, go find and arrest these two white guys because my ghost friend saw them acting dodgy!'"

"Why not? White people are always calling the police on black people!"

"Smith, look at me. I am a Latina woman working in a going-bankrupt bookshop. I will not be taken seriously and have no evidence because I was up here the whole time. If, when, they make a move, well, we'll just have to deal with the fallout."

Amelina left Mx. Smith to ponder on the injustices of the world to get a mop for the drips on the floor. She'd had visions of somebody slipping and the shop couldn't afford a lawsuit.

The rest of the day was punctuated with a wave of customers seeking shelter from the rain. Amelina found the umbrella bucket, kept an eye on the floor for creeping puddles, made eight cups of tea (three sugars between them) and one cup of coffee with a drop of milk, but all the while she was taming the flutter of anxiety that was a constant at the back of her mind. She was loathe to call time at six 'o'clock, and allowed the last two people in the shop to mull over their purchases. But they were considerate and paid up quickly, leaving with promises to come back and tell her how they got on with their chosen books. Amelina switched round the sign to closed, secured the front door and set about the locking up routine, taking care to double lock what could be. Mx. Smith drifted through each section of the shop, morose with heavy sighs, touching their beloved books with weightless fingertips.

The rain eased off just after Amelina fell asleep, tucked up in her single bed. Mx. Smith didn't sleep so much as plunge into oblivion. But they couldn't face that, anxious as they were about their precious books and shop. They sat on the upstairs window seat, tracing water droplet paths down the window.

Mx. Smith was so high strung that they missed the click of the back-door lock being sprung free in the basement. But they couldn't miss the creak of the floor as somebody moved their weight over it. Mx. Smith stopped tracing patterns on the glass, stared at their translucent reflection and made a decision.

They allowed their weightlessness to plunge them through the floor, down through the main shop floor into the basement-office. They took up position by the back door, watching the pair of men - the same from earlier they were sure - busy over the desk drawer. One was busy with picks, the other held a torch, aiming the beam on the lock. They were oblivious to Mx. Smith's presence.

They hadn't really experimented with their death-powers, not really. As far as they were aware they were little more than getting ashes up people's noses and floating through floors. But this was different, this was their final resting place and nobody was taking that away. Mx. Smith took a breath and began creeping into view, making themself seem solid. They fashioned an axe, a long hatchet with a gleaming blade, out of ashes and shadows. They thumped the head on the floor and the two men shot up, the torch beam turning on Mx. Smith.

"Get out!" they howled, and hefted the axe high. The men fled, through the stacks, up the stairs, to the main shop floor. There was a clatter as they dropped the torch and picks, and they started to panic when they saw the secure front door and window-grilles barring their freedom. Mx. Smith took the stairs one at a time, thumping the axe head on each tread, counting down their doom. The pair panting, eyes wide and rolling, fled upstairs, trying to find anywhere to hide. They settled on the customer toilet, throwing the flimsy lock across and sitting in absolute darkness. Mx. Smith teased a chuckle from between their lips and allowed the wisps of their death-axe to blow away in the draught. They paused on the shop floor, stretching out their arms to encompass the whole of the dark, quiet shop and took a deep, greedy breath, drowning in the smell of books.

The next morning dawned bright with a cold edge to it. Amelina arrived earlier than was necessary, fumbling with her work keys to get through the front door. Mx. Smith met her at the door, putting a frozen finger to the young woman's lips, pointing at the torch and lockpicks on the floor. Amelina raised an eyebrow.

"They're in the customer toilet still. You've got them red-handed," whispered Mx. Smith. Amelina took a moment to make sure she was understanding correctly before shutting the front door behind her. Then she picked up the phone, looked at Mx. Smith and whispered, "I trust you," before dialing 999. She waited outside the shop, careful to look normal and as unsuspicious as possible, and went through a small speech for the police. Her heart was beating hard when the police turned up, two white officers, one a broad, huge man with a five o' clock shadow and a tall, lanky woman. They took Amelina's name and a short statement before asking her to lead the way to the customer toilet. The broad officer knocked on the door of the toilet and Amelina held her breath, anxious to get the whole thing over with.

"This is the police. Open the door." There was a frantic whispering and a quiet argument before the door was peeled open. The two would-be thieves were pale and had huge bruised bags under their eyes.

"Have a little trouble, did we?" The officer took his notebook from his stab vest, along with a pen.

"Is it gone?" the shorter thief, the book-buying thief, whispered.

"Is what gone?"

"The maniac with the axe?"

The officers raised cool eyebrows at each other, turning an eye on Amelina.

"We close at six and I was at home by half seven. Nobody is on the premises overnight." Amelina felt annoyance at being questioned when they were with a pair of trespassers in her customer toilet. She banked the fire threatening to overspill in her belly, telling herself that getting angry with the police would get her into more trouble than the men. She put on a small smile.

"I can pull the CCTV footage of my locking up last night, if that would be useful?" The officers agreed that would, indeed, be useful to the chagrin of the would-be thieves. As Amelina was turning to lead the officers downstairs, the male officer piped up, "get us a cuppa while you're at it, love. We didn't get much in the way of breakfast when the call came in."

Amelina stopped and felt a tingle of annoyance settle in her heart. She mustered every iota of self-control she possessed and turned around again.

"How do you take it?" she asked, going for a neutral tone.

"Like my women: hot, wet and milky."

His partner rolled her eyes and mouthed, "I'm sorry" but her silence just added to Amelina's frustration. Amelina headed down to the office to sort the CCTV footage and was overwhelmed by the need to spit in the officer's tea.

"I'm sorry, Amelina. I didn't know you'd receive this sort of treatment. For all my words and experience with gender and the LGBT community, and for all my reading, I'm still looking at the world through a white-person's lens." Mx. Smith sat on the office desk, a pale rose spreading into their transparent cheeks. They ran a hand through their hair, but couldn't quite meet Amelina's eye.

"I should have asked Mr. Issacs to phone the police instead. They would have taken him more seriously. I don't know what to do, how to react. If I'd called him out on his 'cuppa' comment, it would have been the whole 'just being friendly', 'calm down' crap that women get all the time. But then by saying nothing he gets away with it and will keep doing it." Amelina stirred the tea with such force that a miniature vortex spun out of the depths.

"You need to take a stand. Call him out on his bollocks. All it'll take is 'I don't like the way you spoke to me.' He'll try and justify it, you get the 'hysterical woman' treatment and you ask him to apologise, hand over the footage and job's a good'un. Although, I doubt Mr. Isaacs will want to press charges."

"We can only hope he does."

Amelina took up the tea - made in the worst mug she could find - and handed over the CCTV footage. The would-be thieves had ventured out of their cubicle and had settled themselves on the window seat. They stared at the mug of tea with a starving man's look, but said nothing.

"Cheers, love."

Amelina let a moment pass, but decided that this was it, time to draw her line in the sand.

"I don't appreciate being called 'love', or your comments about how you take your tea, either."

"Oh, well, where I'm from that's just the done

thing, everyone's love or sweetheart. I guess you don't have that from where you're from?"

His ignorance choked Amelina silent as her mind fought to think up a suitable, sensible response that wouldn't land her in handcuffs for being threatening, or worse. However, Mx. Smith's guilt manifested itself as a severe drop in the temperature and a biting draught stirred the pages of the books displayed on tiny side tables. A large art book wriggled out of its case and plunged to the floor with a crack like thunder.

"There a window open?" The officer took a sip of tea and then paused with the mug's rim balanced on his lower lip. He wrinkled his nose and went to put his mug down but instead ended up sneezing violently, sloshing hot tea all down the front of his stab vest, all over his thighs. He yelped in discomfort, dropped the mug and managed to step on it, falling backwards, with a jingle of cuffs, onto the carpet.

For a moment, Mx. Smith allowed a small seed of pride to flare like a supernova in their heart before settling down. They stopped the rustling of the books, the draught and even went to replace the beautiful art book back on its table.

"Holy shit," whispered a thief, and his partner pointed at the book floating in mid-air. The room paused a beat as everyone gawped, not quite believing their eyes. All apart from Amelina who was choking with laughter, biting hard on her thumb.

Mr. Isaacs decided to not press charges, mostly because of potential costs and the emotional strain involved. He was perplexed at the embellished tale being told about the haunting of his business.

"I didn't think upstairs had a draught problem. Maybe we don't notice it?"

"I never noticed a draught. It was weird, but-" Amelina shrugged, "just adds to the character of the place."

Mr. Isaacs nodded and smiled a little. The shop door crashed open with a clang of bells and a gaggle of students spilled in, each with a large rucksack. They held a quick, whispered conversation before a lanky, young black woman with dreadlocks stepped forward and cleared her throat.

"Is this the haunted bookstore?" she asked. Amelina and Mr. Isaacs shared a look and a hopeful smile picked at the corner of his lips.

"So I've been told, yes. How can I help?"

"We're from the Paranormal Investigators Society up at the uni. We'd like permission to sweep for this ghost, please. Won't get in your customers' way or anything."

"Well, I don't see why not. Amelina, please will you watch the till while I show our guests upstairs? Thank you." Mr. Isaacs straightened his bowtie and began an impromptu history of the store, the group of investigators taking notes.

"What the actual fudge?" Mx. Smith poked the top of their head through the ceiling.

"I may have accidentally uploaded all the CCTV footage to Youtube and Twitter. Don't you see? If we can spread the word we might be able to get more customers in, stay open, and you won't have to spend eternity in fancy flats, looking at naked people."

"Amelina, that's bonkers but may just work. Seems I have an audience to baffle and intrigue." Mx. Smith slid back through the ceiling, looking a little excited at the prospect of having a whole new audience to interact with. Amelina grinned and looked out the long shop front window, at the gathering storm clouds full of purifying, cold, clear rain.

Five Hundred and Seventy-Seven Miles

The climbing roses are dying. They are all faded shades of red and pink that will wither to grey before too long. As I pass through the kitchen with my garden shears, gloves and sun hat, I catch a glimpse of the calendar on the wall. I pause. Has it really been ten years?

I continue on to the garden. These roses were labelled as "hardy," able to survive winter frosts and we're barely out of September. I cut through brittle stems with a dry crunch with the first pass of the shears.

It's hard to believe that we've been in Germany for ten years now. I won't wonder what would have happened if we stayed: that's what brought us to Germany in the first place.

There's the pop of asphalt as my husband brings the car up the drive. The engine idles for a few moments before falling silent. My shears go *snick, snick*. The cloy smell of decay is heavy in the air. Ten years and we've never phoned home once; no Christmas cards or birthday presents. I stop cutting and my heart squeezes inside my chest. We are such monsters.

My husband rounds the house and plants a kiss on my cheek.

"What's wrong?" he asks, the smile fading from his lips.

"It's been ten years," I whisper, resting the shears point-first on the ground.

"What?"

"Melly." I hoist the shears up, hack at the dried rose bush with vigour. Tears are hot behind my eyes and it's all I can do to not wilt. All he can do is sigh and fold his arms. He passes in to the house and I hear the door to the living room slam shut.

Melly will be twenty-eight by now. I did look her up on Facebook. Her profile picture shows her cheek to cheek with her girlfriend and she's all smiles. I didn't send her a friend request. I think she still lives in the same house and I like to imagine that she's made it her own.

I've had to cut the rose bush down to the bare minimum. The ground is carpeted with dead roses, twigs and slimy leaves that would have turned to mould. It had been such a pretty rose bush and now it's fallen to ruin. I can hear the hiss and crackle of the television as he channel surfs and a little part of me wishes he would just drop dead.

I can't remember whose idea it was in the first place. Let's see what happens if we leave Melly and start life anew. It was decided that we would leave on the eve of her eighteenth birthday, so that when she awoke she would be a legal adult.

We are such monsters.

*

It begins to rain as I duck into the coffee shop. The water streaks down the windows and blurs the outside traffic to dull patches of colour. I'm a few minutes early according to the clock behind the counter, but he's here all the same. He's sat in the corner with a paper folded over his knee. The smell of coffee is rich and delicious in the air; there is low chatter from the other customers. It is cosy in here. I order an overpriced hot chocolate with whipped cream, and approach Daniel.

"Mel, good afternoon." He finishes his article and puts the paper down on the table. He motions for me to sit and I do, shrugging out of my coat. My glasses are steaming up and I rub them on my sleeve to smear them into some sort of semblance of clean. My drink arrives and I begin to spoon off the cream.

"Daniel, I didn't think you liked public appearances." I peer at him through streaky lenses and give a smile.

"Well, we can't all hide away forever, can we?" He gives me a small, almost sad smile in return, and picks up his briefcase and flicks the clips open. I raise an eyebrow.

"Did you find anything?"

"See for yourself." He takes out a manila folder and slides it over the table. I look at it, a lump pushing up from my stomach and lodging itself in my throat. I draw in a shallow breath. My heart starts to pump faster and I don't want to believe what Daniel has found.

I flick open the folder, close my eyes.

"I thought you would be happy?" Daniel takes a sip of his drink, rests the cup against his lips.

"I thought I would be too." I sigh and pick up the top photograph in the folder. On the back in neat black letters is written 'Berlin, Germany, 25/08'. There's a neat little house with a neatly trimmed lawn. There's a fancy car parked in the driveway.

"Everything you wanted is in the folder, Mel. Telephone number, postal address, email…"

"Thank you, Daniel." The cream has curdled in my stomach. I look away from the folder and its contents, try to focus on the price of a tiny cupcake in the glass cabinet. It is crowned in bright pink icing.

"What are you going to do?" He finishes up his drink and replaces his cup on the saucer with a tiny *clack*. I sit there for a few moments, chewing over things in my head. I have a job and a house, found love. Everything is stable in its own way and did I really want to upset that stability by going out to Berlin and confronting my birth parents?

"I don't know Daniel. I'll think it over." I tuck the manila folder into my bag and finish off my hot chocolate in a few scalding gulps.

"Mel, if you need anything, you know where I am." He stands up, knees clicking, and leaves some small change on the table. He leaves without another word and I'm left in my own coffee-tinted daydreams.

*

It's approximately five-hundred and seventy-seven miles to Berlin from London as the crow flies. On a whim I go to Gatwick airport and purchase a ticket to Berlin. Just like that. Is this how they felt when they left me? Just turned up and got on a plane?

I don't have much luggage with me, just a small suitcase with a few days' worth of clothes and a wash-bag. The manila folder that Daniel has given me is nestled under it all, heavy at the bottom of my suitcase. I am surprised when the scales at check-in said that it only weighs five whole kilograms.

As I sit on the plane waiting for take-off, reality begins to catch up with me. What on earth am I doing? I haven't told anybody where I'm going, haven't notified work or my partner of my intentions. I look about the cabin of the aircraft, look at the happy families ready for a holiday and feel a stab of envy through my gut. I busy myself with my seat belt, let out a deep breath as we begin to taxi out and the cabin crew begin to go through the motions of the safety demonstration.

As we coast up through clouds to a comfortable cruising height, I begin to wish that I had taken the manila folder out of my suitcase and brought it onboard with me. It would have given me something to do, given me time to learn who was who and maybe plan on what I was going to say.

Was I really going to go through with this?

I turn to stare out of the window at the cloud-scape and am blinded. My heart is tripping with anxiety and I can't believe that everybody else around me is calm and happy. How could they be? I suck in a few deep breaths, take the complimentary magazine from its pouch in front of me and begin to flick through it. Expensive tat to buy, an article on wine in France, ten things you *must* do in Germany, all mundane, unimportant things.

*

I put my hands on my hips and tip my head to one side. The rose bush is all stems and dry, brittle sap. With a heavy sigh I heft up the spade and begin to attack the roots of the bush. It is a sickly-sweet death.

A car pulls up out front but I pay it no mind. People are always pulling up outside the house and then moving on. I pause in my work as the car-door slams. I look up and freeze. My heart seems to pause in wonder for a few seconds.

She is holding a brown manila folder between her fingers, spectacles pushed up her nose. Hair is pinned in place just-so on the back of her head and her eyes are full of venom that scares me. I put the spade down and take off my gloves, leave them on the path by the rosebush. I want to say "hello" and wave, but my body betrays me and leaves me mute and numb.

She begins the conversation.

"Excuse me, are you Mrs. Woods?" She is angry, her knuckles are white where she is stopping her hands from shaking and her tone is controlled, too controlled, for somebody here just for a chat.

"No, I'm afraid I don't know who that is." My mouth speaks, but my brain isn't engaged. I stare at this young woman with her big coat and her smart shoes. Lying comes so easy still, but how can I lie to this woman?

I know who she is and the knowledge is seeping through my veins, crawling its way to my heart. Perhaps it will poison me and I will drop dead before too long.

"I have here a folder from a good friend of mine and he assures me that you are, in fact, Mrs Woods." She takes a couple of steps closer and I see that she is a few inches taller than me.

She inherited that from her father.

"Excuse me?" I try to look offended but fail. My words come out limp and pathetic.

"You speak very good English, by the way. I'm afraid my German is very rusty, haven't had to use it since secondary school."

That's when my heart stops again. The poison has reached it and is squeezing it to a stop.

"Melly, I don't know what to say." I wish that he was here to back me up; it was his idea after all.

"I want to know why." Melly clenches her teeth together, grinds them, and she's taking big breaths, trying to force down her anger.

"It wasn't my idea," I begin but that line of thought dies as soon as it leaves my mouth. Why did we leave her? I'm not sure. I can't remember: it's been too long.

"I don't care whose idea it was, I care about why you did this. Why would you leave me? Did you get bored of me, is that it? Raised a child for eighteen years and then poof, disappear without a word." Her rage is impressive and terrible. Her face is blotchy with it, but her hair stays in place as do her glasses. Beneath them her eyes glitter with hurt and anger and all I can do is sink to my knees and whisper, "we are such monsters."

Familiar

Mary had been wrapped in dreams of glorious sunshine when the tap-tap-tapping came to her door. She opened her eyes, took stock of her limbs and the ache of her shoulders before throwing back her blankets. Groping for her plain kirtle and her fur lined cap, she kept an ear out for the tapping at her door again. In the dark of her sleeping-cupboard, she prayed under her breath that this was a visitation from the living. She didn't have the energy to speak to anything else.

On her front step she found Elizabeth Thatcher holding a wicker basket to her chest. She had her long woolen cloak and hood covering her hair and some of her face. She looked more wraith than human woman in the cloud-smothered moonlight and Mary wondered if she were still dreaming.

"Elizabeth!" she hissed, "You can't come tapping on my door at this hour!"

"Please, I wouldn't put you in danger unless it was urgent." Elizabeth took a hurried look about her, but the world was in silent sleep. "It's Pickle. He hasn't eaten in two days and won't leave his basket." She hoisted the basket up and a soft mew raised the hairs on the back of Mary's neck. For all they would face if they were caught on her doorstep in the dead of night, Mary could not help the small smile on her lips.

"Pickle? Is this another of your beloved Shakespeare's creations?"

"Yes, as a matter of fact, it is. Please, will you see what's wrong with him?"

Mary opened the door a little wider and let Elizabeth pass into her cramped cottage, scanning the moon-pierced dark before shutting the door against would-be spies.

Pickle was a puddle of skinny shadow on Mary's pock-marked table. He curled up tight as possible, wrapping his tail about his paws and staring at Mary with his round yellow eyes.

"I didn't think you were the black cat type, Liz. What does your father say?"

"My father can go boil his head for all I care."

Elizabeth took a stool and drew it up to the table. She was wearing her green dress with the long sleeves and black fur around the neck. It complimented her brown eyes and always reminded Mary of her beloved forest.

"Such fire in you, Liz. Not an example to make to the likes of me, I'd say."

"Well, you're not a good example for me to follow either so I guess we're even. A woman living by herself? No male relative to take her into hand? The shame of it all!"

Mary laughed and began stoking up the fire, setting pottage to warm through for her visitor and gathered more light in the form of tallow candles for her table.

"Hello Pickle," she cooed to the cat and offered her hand to him to sniff. I am a friend, let me help you, her scent would say. Pickle took a small sniff.

"Has he been to toilet while in his basket?"

"No, he neither eats nor drinks. Just stays like this." Elizabeth took her rosary from within the folds of her dress and began to fuss with the beads, well-worn but still scented.

Mary ran her hands over Pickle, felt his bones beneath her fingertips, noted the way his fur was dull, the little resistance he put up against her. He started to growl when she tried to open his mouth, though, and Mary frowned at his voice.

"Come along now," she muttered under her breath and grabbed him by the scruff of his neck. Pickle went limp, confused by the kitten-familiar of when his biological mother would move him from place to place.

"Don't hurt him!" Elizabeth's voice rang out, her eyes going wide in panic. Mary slipped her fingers into Pickle's mouth and opened it wide enough to peer in. She frowned at the smell, at the thin blood pooling under his tongue.

"Okay poor thing, here we go. This'll hurt." She dipped her fingers into Pickles maw and plucked the lodged twig that had been caught in the roof of his mouth. Pickle yowled then, a wide thin noise that to Mary's ears was an echoing scream of pain, humiliation but also relief.

"Elizabeth, will you fetch a little milk for your wee beastie. It's in a crock in the stream. Pickle will need something to help get his strength back."

"Was only a twig?"

"Yes, just a twig to you and me perhaps, but it could have been his death."

As Elizabeth slipped out to retrieve some milk, Mary frowned at Pickle.

"What mischief was this?" she hissed. Pickle shot her a look of disdain, but it softened into fear.

"Elizabeth's tutor works against you, Blessed. She knows about my...disposition." Pickle flicked his tongue out and licked his nose.

"Lady Gris? But she-"

"She is beholden to the witchfinders, Mary. God this mouth of mine hurts."

"I won't have that blasphemy under my roof, thank you."

"It's not your roof, young lady. You only rent this hovel. You would need a miracle to actually possess property. But heed me, Blessed. The Lady Gris knows of your skills and would root them out. Tread carefully."

"Then who would deliver their babes and treat their sick?" Mary took up the offending twig from the table and examined it closely.

"They don't see it like that, Blessed."

They didn't see a lot beyond their own noses, interests or desire for power, wealth and absolute control. Mary let out a frustrated puff of air and threw the twig into the fire.

"Tell me of Elizabeth's days. Is she happy?"

"Ah, Blessed. Your heart would burst with joy at her happiness. Her lord father indulges her musical talents and she is encouraged to ride and go shooting through the woods. She spends her days in sunshine and comfort. Only her nights leave something to be desired. She would have you for warmth, to whisper to in the dark. She misses you deeply."

"She will be married soon, I suppose?"

"Yes, Blessed. Please indulge me this one question: Do you love her?"

Pickle, like the majority of cats, was patient. He didn't blink as Mary stared into the fire. It was only a few moments before Mary breathed her answer, nodded.

A whisper of footsteps on the grass outside gave away Elizabeth's return. She placed the still-dripping crock of milk on the table and took her stool again.

"He's like a different cat!" Elizabeth's smile filled Mary with bliss, would have brought tears to her eyes if she hadn't turned away to fuss the fire. She placed a little milk in a bowl to warm through for Pickle, served pottage and some day-old bread to Elizabeth. Mary picked at some bread, her appetite ruined by the painful through that Elizabeth would soon be married and taken away. Away from her.

"I hear you have a new tutor."

"Yes! Lady Gris is very clever and patient. With my mother gone, God rest her soul, she is teaching me the expectations of running a household for when I have my own husband. I... This isn't ladylike at all but I do hope we may grow into love. But enough of my future, Mary, will you ever be wed?"

Pickle gave a little hiccup - some may have called it a laugh - which drew Elizabeth's fawning attentions onto him. Mary avoided the question for as long as it took to retrieve the steaming bowl of milk from the fireside. Pickle purred loud and long as he lapped up his milk, he could have nearly fooled Mary into thinking he was a normal cat.

"I doubt it. I have my herbs, my purpose. I am content as I am, Liz. I'm sure you will be very happy." Just not with her, with Mary on the edge of the forest who would protect her and love her. Who would make her happy, who would treat her with the utmost respect as she deserved.

The two young women sat in a companionable silence, watching Pickle drink down a second helping of milk and then set about washing his paws and face.

"It'll be dawn soon. I need to leave." Elizabeth ran her fingertips across the marks of the table.

"I'll look after Pickle for a few days, fatten him up a little before I send him back to you."

"Thank you, Mary. Here, I brought payment with me." From her belt she took a small leather pouch and tipped its contents onto the table, bronze pennies and a few silver coins. Mary took twelve pennies and pushed the rest back to Elizabeth.

"Will you put the crock back in the stream, please?"

"Of course, it's the least I could do." Elizabeth rose from the table, pulling her cloak close around her, tucking the crock into the crook of her elbow.

"Thank you, Mary. Really, truly. Your patience must be sent by God to put up with my visit at such an hour."

"Just stay safe. Watch Lady Gris and be careful." Mary pinched candles dead and cracked the door open a little to check nobody was watching them before letting Elizabeth out. Elizabeth paused on the threshold before leaving, looking into Mary's green eyes.

"Thank you again," she whispered and placed a quick kiss on Mary's cheek before disappearing into the night.

Mary shut the door and lay her forehead against it, shutting her eyes. Her cheek was alight in joy and yet her heart felt like it would break. Tears welled up in heartbreak and love. She clenched her hands into fists and stood like that for a very long time. Long enough to allow Pickle to finish his bath.

"Blessed?" he whispered.

"You listen to me. I am counting on you to keep her safe." Mary turned around, a fire in her eyes that was nothing to do with the banking light in the hearth.

"So am I sworn, Blessed."

"You keep an eye on this Lady Gris and report to me anything suspicious."

"Yes, Blessed."

"I will keep Elizabeth safe and happy, witchfinders or no."

"Yes, Blessed. By the oath I took, Elizabeth will be safe and happy. Now, not to be rude, but could I have some more milk?"

The Joys Of A New Pet

"When you said he'd had a wee behind the sofa I thought it was a little sprinkle, not a full on lake."

"I know, love, and I'm sorry. I think he's still settling in and adjusting."

"Don't be sorry. It can be sorted." Tim placed a feather-light kiss on George's nose. "I'll sort it if you make breakfast?"

"Okay."

Tim had never owned a cat before, he'd had the occasional firework-bright goldfish and a hamster when he was a child, but cats were new to him. He had now learnt that cat wee stank to high heaven through first-hand experience, and the internet was telling him that normal carpet cleaner wasn't going to hack it because if the smell molecules weren't broken down properly then this accident could become a repeat performance.

Tim also read that a black light could show up cat pee marks, especially dried patches that might not smell to weak human noses. So, he left a pile of crumpled paper towel soaking up the crime scene to find his old black light somewhere in the spare room.

"Do you want one egg or two?" George called from the kitchen.

"Two, please," he replied, double-timing back down the stairs.

"What's this for?" George poked his head around the door, mouth-breathing against the ammonia stink.

"Apparently, this will show up cat pee stains. Thought we could tackle any others we may have missed."

"I dread to think what Mrs. Hooper got up to before selling this place. What if the walls are soaked with… fluids?"

"Grim."

"Just remember that what future-you sees cannot be unseen." George disappeared back into the kitchen to carry on with their midweek breakfast treat. Tim, meanwhile, had gone a little cold at George's comment about Mrs. Hooper's clandestine activities. Her whole reason for selling the house, and a little under the market value to boot, was because her husband had disappeared without a trace. The memories held in the brick and mortar were too much for her to handle any more so she moved to the coast to start over.

Tim shook himself and pushed his glasses back up his nose. He had been watching too many true crime programmes again, the kind that made him sleep with a ladle under his pillow to beat off would-be burglars, kidnappers or serial killers.

"Idiot," he whispered and switched on the black light. It's funny how something as little-thought of as flicking a switch can change a life. Tim stared at the black-matt stains that clawed their way up the wall and started to wish he had left well enough alone.

"George," he whispered, hoarse. He cleared his throat once, twice, but found he could not speak. Instead, he followed the void-dark marks across the wall, down onto the carpet. Here they metamorphosed from oblong smears to handprints. Tim's stomach was filled with a fizzing heat as he watched the handprints crawl towards the kitchen door, but they stopped short in an explosion of violence, a wide, spreading patch that chilled Tim to his very heart.

"Breakfast is nearly done. What's wrong, babe? You've gone grey." George folded his apron into a square, coming in from the kitchen. Tim pointed to the handprints, the obsidian-pool of long-dried blood.

"Holy shit," George whispered, taking the horror-light from Tim's numb hands. He flashed it across the floor, towards the kitchen where the trail continued as two long smears.

Tim and George said nothing as they tracked the invisible past through their kitchen and out the backdoor.

The garden was paved by the backdoor but gave onto a semi-wild lawn which fed into a copse of ash and pine. At some point the lovers started holding hands, marching across the lawn, still following the midnight-tinted drag marks. They disappeared into the copse, moving over mulch, root and fallen branch.

And the bottom of Tim's stomach fell out as they came to the end of the ghost-trail, curled in on itself at the free-form compost heap started by Mrs. Hooper years ago. George switched off the black light, the click like a gunshot in the silence.

Extinction

Solstice had a crush on Nicky. They, Solstice, was at first confused by the fat, gender-fluid black person who wore snapbacks and low trousers, because if Solstice was crushing on a genderfluid person, were they then not bisexual? Maybe pansexual was a better fit, they thought as they finished sweeping the storeroom of the small corner shop.

It was ten to ten PM and the summer night was sweltering, still pink around the edges where the sun had not quite set. In another ten minutes, Solstice could leave their apron on the hook and leave. Leave and head straight to Strobe, where Nicky would be playing their new set.

Solstice's heart did a little flip flop and they gave a little giggle and blushed. They caught sight of themself in one of the fridges, stuck their tongue out at their long strawberry-blonde hair, pale skin and full, blue eyes. Were their looks obviously gender-neutral? Mustn't be if every day was an eight-hour shift of 'miss' and 'mademoiselle'. But did it really matter if their looks weren't the absolute stereotype of non-binary?

Well, of course not. Solstice was comfortable in their own body and that was all that mattered.

They gave themself a cheeky wink and went to replace the broom back in the cleaning cupboard.

The bell over the shop floor gave a little tinkle as a last-minute customer waltzed in. Mr. Vong could deal with them, and Solstice took a quick look at their mobile, nestled safely in their apron pocket. No new messages, but Nicky had tweeted a picture of the stage they'd be playing shortly, all neon and shadows. And it'd been Nicky who had personally invited Solstice to their new set, mustn't forget that.

They tucked their phone away, looked about for a tiny job to fill the last eight minutes of the shift.

Raised voices from the shop floor, angry voices. Solstice peered through the one-way glass in the stockroom door, saw Mr. Vong behind the counter, gesturing at the exit, talking over a figure in all-black and Solstice went cold at the sight of the sawn-off shotgun being waved about.

What had they always been told? If anybody staged a robbery, just give them what they want and call the police afterwards. Don't attempt to hit the panic button.

Mr. Vong was so calm, his face tight with anger, not a hint of panic in his features.

"It's not here, I keep telling you. Now get out!"

"Dan said you have it, now hand it over!" The shotgun came up.

"Dan says a lot of things," came the cool reply.

"Fuck you, old man!"

The gun went off and Mr. Vong crumpled to the floor. The robber - murderer? - hopped the counter and began to pat down Mr. Vong.

Solstice felt the blood run out of their face, blinking repeatedly to clear the nightmare in front of them. With heart hammering, Solstice took their phone and dialed the emergency services, a number they had prayed they need never use. Their hands were numb, shaking, but they managed to squeak at the operator and request the police.

"Do you have the necessary insurance for this request, or will you require an alternative?"

Solstice watched with wide eyes as the robber got up from behind the counter and approached the stockroom door. Solstice hung up and leaped at the store cupboard, closing the door with a neat click and crawling behind the tarps hanging up to dry. Clutching their phone to their chest, they strained their ears until they could hear their pumping blood, could hear the scuff of trainers over the wooden floor, the stockroom door banging closed and then a pause. Solstice stopped breathing, closed their eyes and began to pray.

Footsteps moved away, another door opened - the door to Mr. Vong's flat? - and Solstice waited a moment before crawling to the door and opening it an inch. The stockroom was empty so Solstice creeped out of their hiding place, slipped through to the shop floor and had to take a precious second before looking at Mr. Vong.

The pellet had peppered his chest, studding it like cloves in a roast ham. His breathing was a gurgle and as his eyes met Solstice's, he tried to speak.

"No, no, Mr. Vong. Just breathe. I think the police are on the way." They felt disconnected from their body, outside of time almost, especially when they took Mr. Vong's blood-slicked hand. He squeezed like a vice, hurting Solstice and making them gasp.

"Hem, your hem," Mr. Vong choked, his other hand clawing at Solstice's apron. And with a gurgle, a shudder, the life went out of Mr. Vong and Solstice was left alone, kneeling in a coagulating pool of blood, soaking up her knees and shins.

The door tinkled open and Solstice blinked back panic-tears; what if the robber- murderer - had a friend?

But no, they poked their head above the counter and found two police officers in matt-black uniforms, faces shielded by mirror-helmets.

"Burglary! Help! They're upstairs!" Solstice pointed at the stockroom door and the officers stomped through, shouting as they pounded up the stairs. More crashing, screaming, but it felt a long way off.

Solstice squeezed Mr. Vong's hand, bowing their head for a moment. The clatter and crash of the police coming back down the stairs sounded like somebody had fallen down them, and by the look of the murderer, maybe the police hadn't been too gentle with him. Cuffed and hooded, he was marched out to their truck, disappearing into the hold.

The officers took Solstice's statement and let them go with a warning to stay in town for a potential follow-up. Solstice walked home through the dark, empty streets, the occasional drunk party parting and flowing around them without a second look.

The long-mirror on the back of Solstice's front door showed a blood splattered, death-like youth. They began to shake, the events of the evening catching up with them. They stripped off, sat in the shower under a hot, scalding stream of water that blotched their pale skin, until their eyes began to droop and sleep threatened to overtake them. They collapsed onto their tiny bed, tucking the duvet around them to stay safe and warm.

Solstice dozed for a few hours, brain churning over the last day and they snapped awake: Nicky's set! They sat up, clutching the duvet under their chin, and felt hot, shameful tears well up, spill down their cheeks.

How to explain what had happened? Could they explain what had happened? It was still so vivid and bright at the forefront of their mind.

Solstice shivered and pulled their pile of clothes towards them, their apron still sticky with Mr. Vong's handprints. His last words welled up, "Hem, your hem." They pursed their lips and fetched the scissors from their desk, pinched the hem between thumb and finger. In the corner, there was something long and thin. Solstice unpicked the stitching by the light of the desk lamp, found a length of wax paper rolled into a skinny cigarette shape. Unfurled, Solstice was holding a long, thin, dark brown crochet hook, shiny as if oily. Their brain knew this shape, knew it had been important. Solstice lay it down on its wax paper sheath and dug their phone from their apron pocket, threw on their dressing gown.

"Agent, tell me about vanilla," Solstice whispered into their phone. The phone wasn't the most up to date model, was getting on a bit, took a few heartbeats to compile an answer. Agent's robotic trill blared into the hush, Solstice scrambling to turn the volume down.

"Vanilla was once a capricious market commodity which saw extreme fluctuations in prices and supply. Due to climate change and political pressures, vanilla is now extinct in the wild and the flavouring found in foods such as ice-cream is synthetic."

Agent rabbited on, detailing dates, events, people, a whole history, while Solstice stared at the unassuming been on her desk. Was this what Mr. Vong had been murdered for?

Why had he told her about it?

Solstice bit her lip, silenced Agent, and began pacing her room, thinking, brain awhirl. Where did Mr. Vong get a vanilla bean from? And what had he planned to do with it?

Agent twinkled and Solstice glanced at the screen and felt a blush blaze across their cheeks, down their neck, felt the little butterflies twirl and skip in their stomach.

Nicky. Nicky was texting them at 2am!

- Hey missed you

Solstice's breath caught. But what to say? The truth. It'd be on the first news bulletin.

- Hey, hold up at work - robbery gone bad. I'm sorry.

The three little dots on the screen danced, and danced, and danced. Stopped. Stopped for thirty seconds. Was that the wrong thing to say?

Agent twinkled again.

- Shit! Are you okay? Where are you?

- I'm okay, at home. Shaken, in shock? Mr. Vong killed

- I'm coming over

Solstice's whole body set alight with nerves. Nicky? Coming here? They looked about, noting the pile of blood-flecked clothes on the floor, noted their own nakedness under the dressing gown and squeaked.

- Buzz twice when you get here

Solstice lay Agent down like a precious work of porcelain and was set into motion getting dressed, tidying hair, throwing their clothes in the washing machine and then a light came on in their mind: make ice-cream, vanilla ice-cream.

A treat to apologise for not showing up, not supporting Nicky. Solstice ploughed ahead, dusting off their long-ignored ice cream maker that had sat abandoned under the sink, tucked under bin liners, waxed paper and dusting cloths.

Everything was a-whirl, lights were too-bright, brighter than searchlights and the rich smells of cream and full-fat milk, sugar and that silky scent of vanilla as Solstice slipped their knife tip down the bean's belly and scraped the tiny black seeds into the churning bucket. She set the machine to Rapid and went to pace by the front door, furiously clawing their fingers through their hair to try and make it look nice.

Solstice's heart was hammering, but it seemed to stop when the buzzer went once, twice. They let out a shaky breath as they pushed the release button for the front door of the building. They peeped out of their door, listening to the echoing footsteps on the stairwell.

And then, Nicky had arrived. Bald, black, taking up space and loving it, Nicky slipped a thumb under their shirt and fixed their bra strap back in place.

"Hey, you okay?" Nicky took Solstice's hands and squeezed them, worry creasing their face.

"I don't know," Solstice peeped and locked the door behind them.

"You making ice cream? Your machine looks ready to throw itself to the floor."

The machine clunking loudly, beating its soupy contents with a machine gun staccato, hopping towards the counter edge with each revolution of its barrel.

"Yeah, to say sorry for not making it tonight."

Nicky held up a hand to stop the words, shook their head.

"You've been through something tonight, Sol, and there's always next time. Come sit and tell me what happened."

With the background staccato of the ice cream maker getting quieter as the mixture began to set, Solstice sat with Nicky, hands sandwiched between their knees, and began to talk, began to put together what had happened. And there was a slow realisation of what they had done by slipping the tip of their knife down the belly of that bean, the last vanilla bean on earth.

Solstice looked at the ice cream maker, at the little green blinking display: Fin

WORDS ON A WALL
IAN SHARMAN

Monsters, cryogenics, relationships, religion, war, dragons, cannibalism, angels, demons, space exploration, aliens, beans, eyes, traffic cones, gods, Chicago, pot plants, robots, a dive bar on Mars, goblins, heart break, July, cake, bees, geese, peacock flavour crisps and time travel are just some of the things you'll find in this eclectic collection of flash fiction and poetry.

Originally written for the Elephant Words website where writers are challenged to produce a new short piece of writing each week inspired by a picture posted to the site, this series of short stories, scenes and poems charts the musings and preoccupations of award winning writer, Ian Sharman.

At times incredibly dark and deeply personal but often very, very silly.

ISBN: 978-1-911243-20-5

STORIES FROM THE CHICKEN FOOT HOUSE

TINA JACKSON

What are the stories that Baba Yaga reads in her Chicken Foot House?

Take a walk off the beaten path in this collection of grungy fairy tales and discover backstreet clubs and big tops where borderlines blur between the everyday and the extraordinary.

Enter a world of enchantment where wild beauty is waiting to be found in everyday lives and a trip in a rock'n'roll tour bus might be a life-changing ride. Accompanied by Andrew Walker's beautiful, unearthly illustrations, these are tender, quirky transformation tales for readers who would rather wear Doctor Martens than be Disney princesses.

ISBN: 978-1-912700-15-8

WWW.MARKOSIA.COM